the
WITCH
IN THE LAKE

Anna
Fienberg

ANNICK PRESS
TORONTO • NEW YORK • VANCOUVER

Annick Press Ltd.

Cover design by Irvin Cheung/iCheung Design
Cover illustration by Charles Bell
Text design by Sandra Nobles

First published in Australia by Allen & Unwin

Cataloging in Publication Data
Fienberg, Anna
  The witch in the lake
North American ed.
ISBN 1-55037-723-X (bound).—ISBN 1-55037-722-1 (pbk.)
  I. Title.
PZ7.F47919Wit 2002   j823   C2001-903092-4

Distributed in Canada by: Published in the U.S.A. by:
Firefly Books Ltd.   Annick Press (U.S.) Ltd.
3680 Victoria Park Avenue   Distributed in the U.S.A. by
Willowdale, ON   Firefly Books (U.S.) Inc.
M2H 3K1   P.O. Box 1338, Ellicott Station
                                Buffalo, NY 14205

Printed and bound in Canada by Webcom.

visit us at **www.annickpress.com**

Chapter One

"Leo, come back! You're going too close—are you crazy? *Leo!*"

Merilee's heart pounded. She peered through the branches of the tree they'd been climbing. There was the small stick figure of Leo. He was waving his arms, yelling something, marching towards the lake. In the distance he could have been a toy soldier, set to face the enemy.

The ground looked so far away. "We're on top of the world!" Leo had cried only a moment ago—until he'd turned suddenly and whooshed down the tree as if a hurricane were blowing.

Merilee watched the shadows creeping, dark webbed fingers growing longer and thinner as the sun slid down the sky behind her. "The light's nearly gone," she called. "*Stupido!* Do you want the witch to get you?"

Merilee scrambled down from the tree. The breath in her throat was fast and sharp. It almost hurt. In her head there was the song they'd sung since they were babies:

> *The witch will get you, look out, look out,*
> *Snakes in her hair and eels on her chin,*
> *Look now and see what trouble you're in!*

All the village children knew that song. If you sang it loud enough, played games—*"you* be the witch and *I'll* be the child"—if you made jokes about it, why, maybe you'd never meet the witch in real life. Because just to see the witch in the lake, just to glance at her, was enough to steal the power of speech from a grown man.

Merilee ran to the edge of the forest. Her bare feet felt the soft pine needles give way to the pebbly shore. And there was Leo, *his* toes nearly in the water.

"Leo Pericolo, I could *kill* you. *Mamma mia*, what do you think you're doing?"

How *could* he? Ever since they were babies, the mothers in the village had warned them. "Don't go near the lake, little ones—*she* waits there, under the water. When the sky is dark and the moon is full, the witch will come creeping, up, up out of the lake..." and they would cover their mouths and shake their heads at the horror.

Merilee closed her eyes. "See," she remembered her grandmother's whispering, "see how dark with your lids squeezed tight? That's what it's like at the bottom of the lake. So don't go there, whatever you do."

Merilee stared out at the lake. She thought it must be deeper and darker than any in the world. It lay at the foot of the village like a dirty black stain. No fish flashed through its murky valleys. No sunlight dripped through its greasy folds. The lake smelled of dead things.

Leo hated water. Always had. Merilee knew he had nightmares. The lake dripped through his dreams like ink. But for her (and everyone else she knew), the lake was just simply out of bounds, like poisonous plants or deadly fungi. The lake was one of those forbidden and dangerous things, and she accepted that as she knew the sun would rise every day and the moon was too far away to touch. But Leo—well, he'd always been different.

A cool wind sprang up and ruffled the leaves. She saw the shadows tremble on the shore.

"It'll be dark soon, Leo. Please come back, please!"

"Look, Meri," Leo called back. "I think I just saw something. See over to the right, is that something stirring, or is it just the wind making waves?"

Merilee's heart began to race. Her skin felt tingly all over her back and shoulders. "I can't see anything—"

Leo was staring at the water. Then he did something that made Merilee gasp.

"You maggoty old hag," he yelled at the lake, "why don't you come and get me if you're so b-a-a-a-d!"

"Leo!" whispered Merilee.

Leo shook his fist at the lake and its evil ghost.

"Come on," he shouted, "you festering old toad!"

"Stop it!" Merilee raced towards Leo. She tried to grab the hem of his tunic but he was dancing away in the shallows, splashing and punching the air.

"Try and get me, you slimy drop of nose ooze, you weeping sore on the face of humanity—why don't you burst out of there?"

Merilee slapped her hand to her mouth in horror. Far out, past Leo's wicked words, across the dead body of the lake, she saw a silver light rim the horizon. It grew steadily, sending a small ladder across the water.

"Leo, the moon is rising!"

Leo turned towards her. He stopped dancing. "So? It's not full tonight, is it?" For the first time, there was a slight quiver in his voice.

Typical, thought Merilee. He's always in such a rush, so carried away by some feeling or invention, that he never stops to check the details. Little details, like a full moon, down by the lake!

Fear and fury made her want to shake him.

"I don't know. But we're not allowed to be here anyway. You know the law against being away from the village after sunset. It was made to *protect* us, for heaven's sake, and here you are, trying to get us killed!"

Merilee suddenly saw the families of her village, all gathered safely together behind barred doors. The lamps would be lit, the fires glowing brightly. Oh, how she longed to be there, cooking with her mother, helping to roll out the dough for the night's pasta.

The lake was such a desolate place. Travelers always kept to the high road, never daring to come down to water their horses or rest their legs. Even in the daytime, no one came here. There were no summer picnics on the shore, no afternoon strolls. And when the moon was round as a coin in the sky, people drew their curtains against the light, as if the witch's power could ride in on the moonlight and snatch them all away.

Leo never closed the curtains. He would fling open the window and stare out at the twinkling light frosting the leaves of the forest. "I dare you!" he'd shout into the wind. "Show yourself, you warty old witch, and I'll turn you into a worm!"

They both glanced back at the water. Merilee's legs suddenly felt leaden. The wet gritty sand under her feet seemed to suck her down. They watched, stuck like figures in a painting, as the moon rose above the horizon, a perfect, shining circle.

"There!" whispered Leo, and he pointed towards the middle of the lake.

They peered into the dusk. Merilee stopped breathing. A small cut was opening in the surface of the water, as if some invisible hand were making an incision in a body. The water peeled back, like the lips of an ugly wound, and a shape was forming in between, rising up. A moan, like the hungry sound of all lost things, flew on the wind.

"*Mamma mia, santo dio*, run!" screamed Merilee, and she grabbed Leo's hand and pelted up the shore, her feet catching on sharp little rocks and pebbles that she hardly felt. And all the time the moon shone like a beacon over the forest and the moan sang in her ears, the feathery cry of death and lost souls.

"I don't want to hear that, don't let me hear that," panted Merilee as they crashed through the forest, the earth soft and safe beneath them. They whipped their way like snippets of string through the trembling trees, the wind strong at their backs, still carrying the dreadful sound.

"When will it stop? Will they hear it at home? Where will we say we've been?" Merilee still clutched Leo's hand. "They mustn't know we've been together, my mother would go crazy, Aunty will beat me!"

Leo grabbed her other hand and yanked her round to face him.

"We can't stop now, come on. We're so late!" Merilee tried to pull her hands away.

"Merilee," said Leo, so close they could feel the pounding of each other's hearts, "something happened tonight. You want to ignore it? Listen—" and the moan sobbed through the dusk. "It's real, isn't it," Leo whispered, as they stood clutched together against the dark.

Leo's breath was warm on her cheek. He smelled of pears and pastry. He was so dear and familiar, like her own brother. She'd known him forever. She knew his pointy chin and strong, brown wood-chopping arms. She knew that amazing head of silver hair, making him look, since the day he was born, like a very wise and ancient child.

But now he was touched by something else, something foreign, and his voice was full of awe.

"It's always been real, silly," Merilee said, trying to bring him back. "So many people—children!—have disappeared. That's why there are laws. Your own grandfather saw the witch, and he barely survived."

"Yes, I know," Leo nodded impatiently. He'd grown up with that story of old Manton Pericolo, still dreamt of it. Manton had gone into the forest, so the story went, to hunt pheasants with his friend. But they'd been led on, down to the lake, and he'd returned alone, dripping from head to foot. "I could do nothing to save him," he'd wept. Manton was never the same again. His mind had "gone," people said, and he drooled. He was too frightened to swallow, for the rest of his life.

Leo shook the image away. "But all we've ever seen, I mean in *our* lives, is the fear. We've never seen anything real, until now. You know I've always hated it. 'Be home by sunset, don't go wandering near the lake, don't look at the moon.' *Ugh!* This damn fear, it's like a wall keeping

7

us out from the rest of the world. It's as if we're in jail here."

"Well, but it's only *one* place we can't go," Merilee said quickly. "There are plenty of others—"

"Where? Where can *we* go, since we're not allowed to see each other? Oh, I'm sick of it, Merilee. What if the witch has only ever been a story, you know, the nightmare of a poor madman, and we've all become prisoners of it, making laws to keep it out, keep ourselves safe?" Leo threw up his arms. "I just want to see this thing for myself, Merilee, smash that old hellhag and get free!"

Merilee had a sudden glimpse of herself long ago, running through Leo's house, playing hide and seek. *Is he under the bed, in the old chest, behind the big cooking pot?* she'd whisper, laughing, her feet clattering on the stone floor, the tension building in her chest so that she could hardly bear it. And then she'd hear Leo's giggle, from somewhere you'd never believe, and there'd be the rush-tumble as they raced towards the safety of the hearth.

But that was years ago, when Laura was still alive, and Merilee had dashed in and out of Leo's place as freely as if it were her own.

"My own sister," she said quietly.

"Oh, Merilee," said Leo, flinging an arm around her shoulders. He stared at the ground. "I'm sorry, I just don't think, do I?" Leo looked up into her face. "But don't you see, all we've ever really known is that Laura disappeared. We don't know that it was the lake, do we? No one saw. Or at least, no one *told.*" Leo frowned.

"Oh, come on, let's go," Merilee said tiredly, pulling away. "I'll probably be skinned alive as it is. *Dio*, where will we say we've been?"

Leo groaned, but he ran after her, overtaking her, and they crashed through the forest, breaking sticks under their feet and crushing herbs so that the smell of wild mint was everywhere.

When they reached the clearing, where the narrow cobblestone road began, Leo stopped. "I'm sorry, Merilee," he said, panting. "I'm so sorry that we're late and I scared you. I didn't mean to, I didn't think, and now you're going to be in trouble." He pulled at his hair, wondering. "Could you say that you were looking for some plant in the forest to make a potion, you know, something useful that your aunt would appreciate like, like—"

"Like deadly hemlock—I could put it in Aunty's wine!"

Leo gave a crow of laughter. "No, you'd be found out and taken to the gallows and I'd have to come and rescue you, and you know how I'm always late—"

Merilee giggled. Then she held her breath. "Listen," she whispered. "Can you hear anything?"

There was just the dark of the forest behind them and

the soft gleam of the polished stones on the road ahead.

"No, it's gone," said Leo. "I'd better leave you here. Good luck, Meri."

"We'll see each other at the tree, Saturday?"

"Surely. You'd better go now. And Meri? *Lavender.* Say you were collecting lavender."

"*Ciao*, Leo," said Merilee, feeling lighter, but as she went to kiss his cheek, she suddenly stopped. Little prickles of alarm scurried down her back. Leo's face was shining with energy. She could practically see an idea painting itself in bold passionate colors all over his brain. She turned away and began to run towards home, but his voice carried over the stones, clear as a bell tolling.

"We'll hear it again, Merilee," he called fiercely, "and when we do, I promise you it'll be for the last time!"

It will be, for sure, thought Merilee grimly, because no one hears anything ever again from the bottom of the lake. And she shivered deep inside even as she saw the piazza opening like welcoming arms and the church spire shot with moonlight and the warm golden stone of the houses all huddled cozily together. The lake had a voice now, as black and hungry as death, and she could hear it whining pitifully, persistently, deep in her skull, and now that she'd heard it she knew she would never get it out.

Chapter Two

Leo watched Merilee hurry round the corner, into the square. He could imagine her trying to melt into the shadows as she ran. No trace of daylight was left in the sky. He bit his lip. Stars were strewn above him, as if someone had tossed a handful of jewels, like dice, and left them where they'd fallen. Sometimes he felt his life was like that.

The smell of wood fires caught in his throat. Everyone was inside, cooking, eating. He hoped Merilee was almost home. In his mind he saw her so clearly, scampering through the narrow lanes, out of the village and into the fields. The ground would be soft with spring grass, stony in patches. He grimaced. She had further to go, with her house on the outskirts of town. He wished he'd been able to walk her home.

He used to do that, almost every night. Stopped for dinner, too.

Leo braced himself as he thought of his father. Winding through the alleys, his feet sliding silently over the stones, he made up his own story of the last two hours.

"Well, this is a fine time to come home, my boy," Marco Pericolo said, looking up with a start, his voice booming out over the quiet of the house.

But Leo couldn't help smiling. He'd been standing there for five minutes already, and his father hadn't even noticed him. The fire hadn't been lit for supper, and the big iron pot that hung over the hearth wasn't yet filled with water for their *minestra*.

When Leo crept in, Marco had been huddled over his notebook, glancing feverishly at sheets of paper scrawled with diagrams of the human body. He'd been making frantic notes, muttering to himself in excitement, sharpening his quill and saying *"si, si!"* every few seconds.

Marco saw the smile and grinned sheepishly back at his son. He waved in the direction of the fireplace and shrugged. "The thing is, Leo," he said, "there's so much work to be done. Important work."

Leo nodded. He began to bundle up the kindling and dried leaves.

"See, I've got hold of this extraordinary manuscript. You should see some of the drawings."

Leo chose a log and placed it on the fire. He looked up at his father's face. His dark eyes were sparkling with lamplight and his silver hair was curling up in wiry spirals where he'd been winding it round and round his finger. Merilee had often said that Leo was just like Marco.

It was true, thought Leo, looking at him now, we can talk about anything—anything except Merilee and the witch in the lake.

"I've never seen this before, Leo." His father swung round his chair to face him. "Probably almost no one has. Look, here are the little vessels of the heart. Can you imagine? The diagram shows what it looks like, right inside a human heart. Come and see!"

Leo came and pored over the drawings with his father. He'd let him talk, he decided, and marvel with him, and soon Marco would forget that Leo had ever been late and then they'd get hungry and eat and add more wood to the fire for the morning, and Leo would go to bed. From his dark corner of the room, behind the tapestry curtain from Florence, he'd hear the sounds of late-night Marco—the whispering, the trickle of the water being added to his glass of wine, the riffling through pages.

Marco never went to bed before dawn. He'd done that ever since Leo was a baby, when his wife had died of fever, and Marco had begun a life's study to find out why.

Leo's father had been born with silver hair. It was the first sign of wizardry, and it ran in all the males of the

13

Pericolo family, just like brown eyes or bad temper runs in others. Marco told Leo that he was a wizard on his fifth birthday.

"Good," said Leo. "Are you a wizard too?"

"Yes," said Marco. "But I was never a very good one. I don't have the twin signs, and then...I think you'll be a much better wizard, Leo. Maybe, one day, you'll be as good as my grandfather. He—" Marco frowned suddenly and raked his hand through his thick bush of silver hair. "Anyway," he went on brusquely, "let's not dwell on the past—we've got your future to think of, my boy. I'll teach you the little I know, and guide you as you grow."

"I'll be a better wizard than *you*?" asked little Leo in wonder. He looked at his father with the big face he couldn't even hold in his hands, and felt a shiver of delight.

Then his father had taken him by the shoulders and looked deep into his eyes. "My magic is weak," he said. "It's untutored and without power—I have never saved anyone. But you, Leo, you will be different. You have the two signs of wizardry, my boy—silver hair and golden eyes. You have the sun and moon within you."

Leo often remembered that day. The day his father had told him about the two signs, the way he'd looked into his face. "You can do anything," he'd said, making Leo's stomach rumble with pride and terror.

Since then, Leo had often comforted himself with

those words of his father's. Because it was hard to keep faith. The exercises they practiced every Thursday were hard and often boring. For a whole hour, sometimes, Leo would have to sit on the wooden stool, staring at an object so that he "understood its true nature."

On Leo's seventh birthday, Marco told him that the Pericolo family specialized in a particular brand of magic—the magic of Metamorphosis.

"That's where one thing is changed into something else altogether," Marco explained. "It's perhaps the most powerful kind of magic. It can create all that is good, but it can call into being the most unimaginable evil." Marco's face closed in then, darkening around some secret storm.

Leo had stared into his face. "Tell me."

They were hunched close together at the table, sharing the circle of lamplight, and their long shadows had danced across the walls. Leo kept silent, holding his breath, desperate with wanting to know. He could see there was some private landscape behind his father's eyes—a time before he, Leo, was born, and Marco had had this whole other life, where maybe, just once, he'd touched evil. "Tell me," he whispered again.

But Marco shook himself, making the shadows shudder. "There's nothing to tell," he'd said abruptly. "But I'll warn you, Leo. Although you may go way beyond me with your magic, you must always stop when

I tell you. You must listen to me. I don't have the power you do, but I have the years and the wisdom to know—"

"What?"

"To know the places you mustn't go, the forests of wizardry that are too dark to explore."

Leo didn't answer. He felt hushed, in awe, as if someone had touched his naked back with a drop of ice.

"You must always obey me," Marco said. "Otherwise you will get lost. Is that understood?"

Leo had nodded. He had never seen his father so serious. His voice was deeper, so certain—it didn't jangle with outrage or passion the way it often did. And strangely, from then on, Leo found the lessons more interesting, absorbing even, and hours floated by while he sat, mesmerized on his stool, his mind traveling to other places entirely.

To practice the art of Metamorphosis, Marco told Leo early on, you have to be able to see.

"Well, of *course!*" Leo laughed. "What do you think I am, an idiot?"

"No, I don't," smiled Marco. "But there are ways of seeing, son. In order to transform something, you have to *see* it first. You have to look straight to the heart of that thing, before you can change it."

"You mean if you only see its outside, then only that will be changed when you do the spell? I mean, it will *look* changed, but the heart of the thing will be the same."

Marco gave a little jump of excitement. "Yes, Leo, that's it, *bravo!* The object's real nature has to be understood, all its history, its deepest soul, even the making of it, has to be seen and held in your grasp. Once you do that, you may learn to change its deepest nature. And then, Leo, you will be practicing the Metamorphosis of the Pericolo family."

Leo glanced around the room, thrumming his fingers on the table. "What about Pidgy? Could I change him, say, into a wolf?"

Leo's pigeon, which he'd rescued in the forest two years ago, perched on the arm of a chair. He blinked back at Leo, as if amazed at the suggestion.

"Consequences," said Marco. "Think of the consequences first. Ask yourself, what will happen if I do this? Would I rather have a pet wolf? Should I take the power of flight from my good friend?"

Leo watched Pidgy flutter his wings. "Oh, no," said Leo, in sudden horror. "Pidgy would hate being a snarly, earthbound creature. Oh, Pidgy, I wouldn't do that to you," and Leo put out his finger for the bird to perch upon.

"One of the first things to learn," said Marco, his voice suddenly deep and heavy, "is that you never use your power for its own sake. It's not a toy to be played with—and you must never discuss it with anyone. It... annoys some people."

Leo stared at his father.

Marco sighed, spreading his hands. "There are very few of us. And the authorities fear magic. The Church says we are devil worshipers—"

"But that's silly—"

"*We* know that, but the consequences of being discovered, Leo, could well be death."

There was silence for a moment and then Marco leaped up to close the shutters. "I think it will take many years before you'll have the power to perform transformation. And I pray to God that by then you will have the wisdom to use it well."

Now that Leo had started looking, he found it hard to stop. He practiced "seeing" everywhere, not just on the wooden stool near the fireplace. To his delight, he found it easy. Without even trying, he discovered new worlds nestled inside such familiar things. He saw trees that remembered the wind in their branches inside firewood and benches and shelves. He saw little boys curled up in men's hearts; a disappointing dream in the eyes of his neighbor. Soon it came as naturally as his next breath. But sometimes it was almost too much. He saw double, triple of anything that other people saw—his mind became crowded, his eyes flooded with private truths. Secrets lay there before him like landscapes behind a fog, and he only had to breathe on them for the cloud to clear.

Chapter Two

When Leo was eight, he went with his father to visit
a merchant who sold brooms. Marco was looking at a
fine, thick straw broom, when Leo whispered into his
ear. "There's a hungry wolf in that man's heart. When he
smiles, I can see its teeth bared to bite." Marco, who had
no money to spare, and didn't want to get bitten,
decided not to do business with the merchant, and later
bought a good, cheap broom on his travels to the city.

Marco was very pleased with Leo. "I knew it," he
exclaimed. "You have great talent. Your vision is your
strongest magic. I've only had a thimbleful. You have a
river. Just like your great-grandfather—"

"Who, not Manton?" Leo shuddered.

"No, *his* father—Illuminato—he had the twin signs,
too."

"Did he look like me, what magic did he do?"

But Marco waved his hand. "Let's walk quickly.
Tonight we'll have supper early, because tomorrow I
must leave for Florence at dawn." He rubbed his hands
together at the thought of it.

Leo never heard all the history of the great Illuminato, and it is a pity because if he'd known more about
him, he might never have thrust himself into danger,
unarmed and ignorant, in the years to come.

Leo's village was quite a distance from the great walled
city of Florence. Most days except Sunday, Leo waved to

his father as Marco set off for the two-hour walk to the city. Only a few of the men from the village worked in Florence, in the busy workshops where they sold wool and silk, cut hair, made looms, built furniture. Most villagers thought it too far to venture, and preferred to stay within the slow secluded world of the village, working in the olive groves and vineyards, or preparing the pig meat for market.

Marco was a wood carver and worked in the back of the shop owned by Signor Butteri. When he was younger, Signor Butteri did his own carving and selling, but now he suffered from gout—a disease that caused his legs to swell and his temper to sour. He couldn't get to the shop so often any more, but he was fond of his assistant, and enjoyed seeing him when he could, because Marco often had a new remedy to try for his illness, and was always interested in discussing his latest symptoms. Even though Marco was sometimes late to work, he was an excellent carver. The workshop specialized in wedding chests, where brides placed their linen, and Marco's chests were very popular, with their smooth satin finish and careful decoration.

Marco quite enjoyed wood-carving—it was a living, he told Leo—and it allowed him to roam about in the city he loved most.

Marco finished work at three in the afternoon. But he

never walked straight home. He lingered. He liked to talk with people—merchants, apothecaries, lawyers, laborers—and hear the heartbeat of the city. He'd drink a glass of wine at the markets, visit the other workshops where artists were painting or sculpting or inventing. The bustle of Florence was so different from the secretive stillness of the village. Marco liked to listen to people's news, and news about medical discoveries was his favorite kind.

Marco was like a detective, searching for clues that would help him solve the mystery of the human body. He wanted to know how it looked inside, how the blood flowed in the veins, how the bones stayed attached and didn't float all about. If he'd had to remain in this small village all his life, he often said, he'd go to the grave believing that the arrangement of the planets above caused the plague down here on earth.

"In the city of Florence, men are searching for truth," he'd sigh. "Here, there is only superstition and fear." And that never saved anyone, he'd mutter to himself.

When Marco came home late from work, he was often lit up, as if he were a lamp someone had kindled. He glowed with hope, talk, new information. "This is a wonderful time we're living in," he'd beam to Leo. "We are discovering so much—it seems every day we know more about life, about *us!*"

And Leo would beam back, knowing he was about to

hear news that belonged only to a handful of people in the country.

In Florence, only twenty years ago, there had lived Marco's hero, Leonardo da Vinci. Leonardo was best known for his art, but Marco was more interested in his investigations of the human body. The great man had kept private notebooks—no one knew how many; most people knew nothing about them at all—and he'd sketched drawings, made notes, scribbled ideas that had never been thought of before in the history of the world.

Leo had stayed up with his father many nights until dawn, when Marco had just returned from the city. He'd tell Leo how he'd got talking with someone, a scholar who'd known another, whose father had assisted the great Leonardo.

"The man had a passion for truth," Marco would begin in a hushed, awed voice, "and he didn't care what danger that put him in." Leonardo had opened up human bodies, Marco said, to study them.

"Ugh!" cried Leo. *"Che schifo!"*

"Well, he wanted to get the anatomy right," Marco explained. "How can you draw a leg properly, with all its strength and power, if you don't know how it looks inside? What's under the skin, how does the muscle pull? So you know what? Leonardo went to hospitals at night, with a lantern, and dissected corpses. He'd cut open the body, and draw what he saw inside."

Leo, listening to this in the flickering light, couldn't help shuddering. He'd looked at his own leg, tracing the muscle under his skin.

"He even followed criminals on the day they were to be executed, to see their faces and how they looked at the point of death. But then," and Marco's face darkened, "the Pope stopped him cutting up bodies. Leonardo wasn't allowed to even set foot in a Roman hospital any more—or he'd be sentenced to death." Marco snorted. "Didn't he just want to discover the truth? Who else ever had the courage to do it!"

Marco kept his own notebooks in a locked box under his bed. He faithfully recorded conversations he'd had, word for word, with people in the city. He'd copy drawings, and compare them with others he'd made, trying to build up his own library of knowledge about anatomy.

But on the night that Leo came home late, with the ghostly echo from the lake still throbbing in his head, Marco was perhaps the most excited that Leo had ever seen him.

"This is truly amazing," Marco was exclaiming to himself as he tried to copy from the sketches lying in front of him. "The human heart on the table."

Leo silently cheered. Wasn't it lucky that Marco's

remarkable discovery had occurred on the very same night as his own? But as Leo built up a fire, and filled the pot with water and slices of turnip and onion, he felt a tug of anger that *his* discovery could never be discussed, whereas the next two hours would be devoted to Marco's.

"See?" Marco thrust a drawing into the lamplight. "This is a copy—but a person who I won't name told me it's a faithful copy of a sketch made by Leonardo some twenty-five years ago. It's only just been found." Marco wiped his hand over his face. "If we know what's inside us, we can find a cure when the sickness comes!"

Leo peered at the drawing. There was a cluster of wiggly lines inside the heart, and lots of tiny arrows and writing that all looked like it was written backwards.

Marco chuckled as he watched Leo's puzzled face. "Mirror writing," he explained. "Leonardo wrote like that for secrecy." Marco picked up a small lady's pocket mirror from the table, and held it close to the drawing.

"He's done cross-sections of the heart," murmured Marco. "You can see all the cardiac vessels. Leonardo says it's the heart that pumps the blood all around the body! What do you think of that?"

Leo had a turn with the mirror, and was excited too when real words leaped out of the jumble of mirror writing. But even as he looked and admired, he wished he could talk about what went on *inside* his heart, and not just about the look of it.

"I think I'll go to bed, Papà," he said at last, and got up wearily from the table. But Marco was still under the spell of the drawing. Leo was putting on his nightshirt when Marco finally looked up and answered him.

"What? You're going to sleep already?"

Leo pulled the curtain back.

Marco looked like someone who has been under-water, coming up suddenly for air. "You're not having any supper, Leo? *Is* there any supper?"

Leo sighed. He watched Marco trying to remember something as his mind came slowly back into the room, into the present.

"*La minestra,*" answered Leo. "You know, the soup—onion and turnip. But I'm not hungry."

"Why? Don't you feel well? What is it?" Marco was alarmed. All at once he was on his feet, coming over to feel Leo's forehead.

Leo grinned. If he'd ever wanted his father's whole attention, Leo had only to mention a slight headache, a sore throat, a stomachache, and Marco would be there, bending over him, consulting his notebooks for treatments. "No, no, I'm fine," Leo waved his hand away.

Marco straightened up. His face was set.

He's remembered, thought Leo.

"Did something happen tonight that made you so late?" asked Marco. "Or were you just careless?"

Look at him wanting me to say the second thing,

thought Leo. *He has to ask the first, but he doesn't really want to know.*

Leo struggled. He imagined those little vessels of his heart wriggling around in confusion. "Something happened, Papà, down near the lake," he burst out.

"Oh, Madonna!" cried Marco, stamping his foot. "How many times have I told you not to go there? A hundred, a thousand? Are you deaf, boy?"

Leo jumped up in rage to face him. "But *why?* You're always saying how stupid these superstitions are. You don't believe them all anyway! Why should we obey these silly laws when it might be just another story—I've heard you say just that!"

"Yes, but the lake—"

"Like the crazy people who believe Massimo's beads ward off the evil eye."

"I know, and now everyone wants them. But the lake is different—"

"And even your Signor Butteri," Leo went on, "last week when his son was ill, he replaced all his furniture with red, because he was told that would cure his son!"

Marco laughed. "You're telling me—I had to go out and find all the new coverings!"

"You admire your Leonardo so much because he *didn't* believe these fanciful ideas, don't you? He did his own experiments. He wanted to discover what's true, right?"

"'Those who only study old books and neglect Mother Nature will never find the truth they are seeking.'" Marco brought out Leonardo da Vinci's words in his serious, deep voice.

Leo nodded. He began to pace around the room in his nightshirt. He felt flushed, excited, as if he were on the edge of a discovery. "So Leonardo relied on experience for his knowledge, yes? He even cut bodies open to see with his own eyes! He didn't just believe what people say."

Marco frowned as his eyes moved around the room, watching his son. "Mm, but the lake is something else, Leo, and you know it. You won't get around me like this."

"What do I know about the lake? Only what people say. Why do *you* believe them?"

Marco looked away. He stared at the wall, where a painting of his wife was hung.

Leo waited, his heart pounding.

"I'll only say this," Marco's voice was loud in the still room. "You must never go near that lake again, my boy, and I hope you didn't involve Merilee in this dangerous adventure of yours tonight—"

"Well, if you want to know—"

"I don't." Marco waved his hand. "Heaven knows we've caused enough sorrow to that family. Just keep away—from the lake and Merilee."

Marco turned his back on Leo and moved towards the table.

Leo let out a grunt of anger. "Are you still dwelling on that? Laura disappeared three whole years ago! It's Meri's aunt who's responsible for all that mess! You tried to do everything you could!"

Marco sat down heavily in his chair. "I did try, but it wasn't good enough. And sometimes that's worse than doing nothing at all."

Leo watched Marco pick up his notebook and begin to read. But he saw his father's eyes hold still, staring off into the dark space of the room. He could only imagine what it must have been like to live through every second of that last hour. Because Leo hadn't been there. No one had—only Marco, who had never said a word.

Chapter Three

Leo and Merilee were nine years old when Laura fell ill. She'd just had her thirteenth birthday, and Leo remembered Merilee telling him huffily that Laura had gone and grown up overnight and wouldn't play games with them any more—not even hide and seek.

"Soon she'll be married to some rich, handsome lad, don't you worry!" her mother said, and Laura had grimaced, blushing.

The day after Laura's birthday, a band of troubadours came to Florence, and they put on a play in the square. Most of the village came to see it, and Signor Butteri made space in the front for Leo to get a better view. ("Don't stand too long with those legs of yours," Marco warned him, but Butteri was in a particularly good mood and asked if Marco had another pair of legs he could stand on.) Afterwards, there was music and one of the young troubadours asked Laura to dance. The musicians strolled around with their lutes and piccolos, and singers lifted their fine voices in pure harmony as Laura and the young man flew around the square, their feet hardly seeming to touch the cobblestones.

It was Marco who first noticed the high color in Laura's cheeks. Her mother thought it was natural, due to all the exercise, but Marco saw how even when she sat and rested, the scarlet in her cheeks didn't pale, and the fine pearls of sweat on her forehead didn't dry.

The next day, it was clear that Laura had a fever. She shivered with cold and sweated through a pile of sheets. Any food she took came up only minutes later. And when her Aunt Beatrice, changing Laura's nightclothes, felt a swelling in her neck, she cried out in terror.

"The Black Death!" she screamed, running into the yard, making the hens squawk and jump, and the pigs squeal with fright. Merilee's mother told her to hush, but her hands shook as she poured water over the cloth to soothe her daughter's forehead.

Leo knew all about the plague that had swept like a hurricane over the country—two hundred years ago Pope Clement had announced it left half the world dead. The sickness had never really disappeared. People still told stories about infants crawling over their mothers' dead bodies; towns deserted and strewn with corpses, with only the rats left alive, wolves living in houses where all the people had died. And every now and then the illness returned—a fever ending in death, perhaps a chill or vomiting, and people would start to whisper and tremble all over again.

In Leo's own village, almost two-thirds of the people had died of plague. Over the decades, priests had cut their monthly visits so that now they were lucky to see a man of the Church once a year. (Although Leo sometimes wondered if it weren't the fog of horror drifting over the lake that kept the priests away, as much as the small number of villagers.)

It was an ever present fear, Leo knew, fear of the plague, and he couldn't sleep with the worry of it.

Leo was worried about Laura, surely, but perhaps he was even more anxious about Merilee. No one had discovered what caused the Black Death, but everyone knew it was catching. So often they'd heard that one person in a family was sick and then it was only a matter of days before the others in the same house were struck down. The great surgeon, Guy de Chauliac, said that the grand meeting of Saturn, Jupiter and Mars, in the sign of Aquarius, had produced the Black Death. Leo's father looked skeptical when he heard that. Others looked at the sky fearfully each night.

All Leo knew was that he wouldn't want to wake up every morning without Merilee in the world.

Leo and Merilee were born on the same day, within minutes of each other. As toddlers, they often slept in the same little bed for their midday nap, when Marco had to work in the city, and Merilee's mother looked after them. They drank their milk and ate their *pappina* together, and Leo taught Merilee to fight like a boy. Out in the yard, they'd wrestle and laugh at the dogs barking hysterically and the hens flapping away until someone would yell for them to come inside immediately and clean up or there'd be no dessert for lunch, and all when Mamma had made a *torta di albicocche*, an apricot tart! They shared the same tutor, too, who was a bit too fond of his wine, and when he fell asleep over their books, they'd sneak out and race into the forest to climb trees.

Leo and Merilee were as close as two peas in a pod until Laura fell sick, and everything changed.

The first morning of Laura's fever, Leo came over and refused to leave. He insisted so passionately that Merilee's mother finally made a bed up for him outside, on the *loggia*. It was summer, and baking hot, and Leo said he didn't need a roof. Marco wasn't happy about it, but he understood Leo's decision.

Marco read everything he could about fevers and chills. In the city, he asked all the doctors and people he knew if they'd heard of any new cures, any new ideas of how to treat the illness. But it was hard to actually get near Laura, what with Aunt Beatrice bent over her every minute.

Aunt Beatrice kept the iron cooking pot boiling all

day over the fire. She boiled up potions of cabbage leaves, mashed and sprinkled with garlic. She strained juniper and dandelion infusions for Laura's aching bones. She and the doctor talked in low voices and tried immersing her in aromatic baths. The doctor suggested a good bleeding, with leeches, but Aunt Beatrice disagreed. She was a Wise Woman, with a certificate from the High Order, and all her Wisdom lay in her knowledge of plants, and the medicinal potions they yielded. She believed in nothing else.

Once, when Leo and Merilee were little, they took a knife and both made a cut in their middle finger so they could mix their blood. When they put their fingertips together, they swore they would always be friends, and save each other in time of trouble. Leo had felt a blazing joy, seeing the drops of scarlet meet and mingle until neither of them knew whose blood it was that pooled in their hands. But Aunt Beatrice had caught them.

"You filthy devil!" she screamed at Leo. "What's this—some demon witchcraft of yours? Get away from her!" and even though Merilee protested, she sent Leo off and made Merilee wipe her fingers with fresh roots and garlic, and stand in the yard with her hands above her head for an hour, so that the blood would leave the poisoned area.

From that time on, Leo knew he had an enemy. Aunt Beatrice was one of the people his father had mentioned long ago—the ones who were "annoyed" by wizardry.

A bed was made up for Aunt Beatrice now, too, right next to Laura. She made the sick girl swallow all kinds of infusions, but nothing ever stayed down. After three days, her fever had worsened. The family were becoming desperate.

"I think we should try opium leaves," Beatrice suggested. "At least that will send her to sleep, and let her body rest."

But while she slept, Laura called out in terror, seeing monstrous things in the dark.

"She's delirious," Aunt Beatrice moaned. "Her mind is failing."

That night Merilee's mother decided to call Marco. He came out in his nightshirt. Leo remembered thinking he'd look funny if only this was about something else. His sandals flapped at the heels and he'd put his hat on backwards. Leo ran out with them, and when they arrived back at Merilee's house, she was at the door to meet them.

"Aunty won't have it," she told them. "She said she won't have any wizards doing their demon work in her house."

Leo looked about fearfully lest anyone should hear. The Church dealt swiftly with someone accused of wizardry. Leo didn't want his father burned at the stake.

"Laura is not *her* daughter," Merilee's mother said

grimly, and marched inside. But Aunt Beatrice was in a towering rage and she blocked the door with her body, as if they were executioners about to cut off her niece's head.

"Francesca," Marco said to Meri's mother in a low voice, "you know I want to help in any way I can. But my magic has never been strong. I...I can't trust it. And even if my power is kindled, I don't know that I can control it. A little magic is a dangerous thing—I've seen what it can do, the despair it can bring."

"Let me try," cried Leo. "What about me? You said I had the twin signs."

Leo's heart burned in his chest. His favorite daydream had always been of saving Merilee. So many nights he'd imagined her in danger—attacked by a wolf, set upon by robbers—and he would leap in and rescue her, whirling a sword around his head.

"No son, you're too young. You need years more practice."

Francesca put her hand on Marco's arm. "I understand your fears. Thank you for being so honest. But we don't have any choice. Look at her. Only some kind of miracle can save her."

Through the frame of Beatrice's arms and hips, Marco saw Laura tossing on the bed. Her hair was wet with sweat and her mouth was moving as she wrestled with shadows.

"Well, I can't do anything here," muttered Marco. "Not with that woman cursing me. I'll have to take Laura away."

In the end, it took all of them and Merilee's father, who had to threaten Beatrice with the farmyard ax, to persuade her to stand aside.

And that is how Marco came to be the last person to see Laura alive.

Chapter Four

Leo couldn't sleep. When he closed his eyes, he could see the moonlight through his lids. It sank in pools into the hollows of the bedclothes—on his feet, above his knees. The pearly shine had a voice. It rustled and breathed at him from those intense, white puddles of light.

Whooo, pheye, moaned the moonlight, and the hair on Leo's neck rose stiff and prickly, and wouldn't lie down.

At three o'clock in the morning, Leo went to close the shutters. He drew the curtains against the light. Marco snored and turned over. Leo thought how surprised he'd be to see his son doing those silly things the other villagers did. Those rituals of fear.

But Leo believed in the witch now. He'd seen something. And he'd heard her. He could feel her presence deep inside him, behind his eyes, where the blood ran. He could feel her moan stroking his bones, creeping in, under his flesh. She made him ache.

When he closed his eyes and turned on his side, his brain wouldn't quieten. Words spelled themselves out in his head. *Demon witchcraft, twin signs...* The words snaked through winking red fireworks behind his eyes. *Forests of wizardry, lake of death, help me.*

Leo turned over and buried his head in the pillow.

> *One two three four*
> *Who is knocking on your door?*
> *Is it the doctor with his bill*
> *Or is it the Witch come to make you ill?*

Leo tried to think about something else—Latin verbs, the bun he'd had for breakfast, Leonardo's heart. But there was the voice behind everything, like an undertow in a river. It rushed his thoughts on, heading always towards the black hungry mouth of the lake.

So many questions, so many mysteries—they kept pushing at him, breathing on him, like the soft wings of a million moths. As he sank down into sleep, he dreamt he was falling into the lake, plunging beneath layers of warm dark water, thick and oily as blood.

The next morning Leo woke late. He didn't even hear Marco leave for work. He got out of bed and put some more kindling on the fire to warm his milk. It was gray outside, the sky lumpy and soiled like an old mattress.

Leo yawned, numb with tiredness. He sat on the

edge of his bed and sipped the steaming brew. He felt smudged, as if someone had come along with a cloth and half rubbed him out. The milk burned his throat.

Today he was supposed to learn his Latin and practice Metamorphosis. How do you concentrate when you're not all there? he wondered bleakly.

"Choose any two objects you like for the lesson," Marco had told him, "providing they are not alive nor valuable. I want you to take notes on your progress, and show me when I come home."

Leo decided to do his Latin first. He'd take his books into the forest and study in the fresh air, in the shade of the trees. Maybe he'd stay there all day, and choose his two subjects for transformation from the forest. A leaf perhaps, a stone. He wondered if he'd have to be ninety-nine before his father allowed him to practice on a live subject.

But all the while he said his Latin words out loud and looked at his leaf, there was a voice floating on the air, faint as a sigh on his cheek, *whooo, pheye.*

When Marco arrived home, late, as usual, showering Leo with apologies and news and enquiries about dinner — Leo was able to show him two pages of Latin, and twenty of magic.

"What's this, just *Gallia est divisa in partes tres*—Gaul is divided into three parts—oh, Leo, this is baby stuff. We learned that years ago!"

"I know," sighed Leo. "I just felt so tired today, it was hard to concentrate. And Latin is so..."

"Latin is the language of learning, my boy. Anything worth reading is written in Latin. Imagine if you can't read the best books—you'll be shut out from the world!" Marco frowned. "Why are you so tired? Do you feel ill, have you got a headache?"

Leo grinned. "No, Papà—but look, look how far I got with the transformation."

Marco bent over his son's notebook. He nodded. "Your depth of vision is splendid. You are ready to go on. Do you have any questions about the second stage?"

Leo hesitated. He studied his father. "I do have one question."

"Yes?"

"Well, I can't stop thinking about our conversation last night," Leo began in a rush. "You know, about Laura, about how you tried to help her. You've never told me," he said more softly, "where you took Laura that night."

Leo could feel his breath sharp in his chest. In the long silence he almost hoped Marco would ignore him and pretend not to have heard the last part of the question. They had never spoken about Laura. Leo knew Marco's mind slithered away from it like a lizard creeping under a stone.

"To the place my father took me," Marco said quietly. "The place his father took him."

Leo swallowed. "Where's that?"

"A cave in the forest. It's quite deep. No one disturbs you."

"Did you practice magic there?"

Marco closed his eyes.

"Why haven't you ever taken me? Like *your* father did?"

Marco stood up suddenly, jolting the table. He turned to face his son. "Because my magic failed there, that's why. It used to shine with power, that place. My grandfather—"

"Illuminato."

"He would hold up a finger, you know, just point to the walls and make you see things: ghosts of animals, fire, people dancing in the stone. It would glow with a golden light, and you felt powerful just looking at it, letting it seep behind your eyes."

Marco's face was alight with memory. "Oh, Leo," he whispered, "Illuminato could make *miracles.* If you only knew, could have seen how he was—"

"Tell me."

Marco threw up his hands. "He could change the nature of disease—transform it! He rescued the dying from the jaws of death. Just a glance from him—"

"Is that true? Was he really such a great wizard?"

"Yes." Marco smiled. "This is no story, son, no silly superstition. I saw it with my own eyes. People in the village came secretly to him at all times of the day and night. They brought him their sick children under the cover of dark. He always helped, and the villagers felt safe, just having him there at hand until—"

"What?"

"Until he stopped."

Marco turned back to the fire, and Leo's rush of questions choked in his throat. He recognized the set of Marco's face, the full stop of his mouth. Leo waited, watching the fire with his father.

When Marco spoke again, his voice floated quietly over his shoulder. It was hushed with awe, as if the things he was about to tell had only happened yesterday.

"I remember when my little friend Domenico fell desperately ill with the smallpox."

"How old was he, were you?" asked Leo.

"Oh, five, I think, or six. Dom's mother brought him to the house of my grandfather. We were there, my father and I, having lunch. Domenico was so sick, covered with terrible boils—he looked as if he had already died, lying there in his mother's arms.

"Illuminato leapt up straight away. He led them in. My father was scared. I saw him clutch at Illuminato's arm, trying to pull him back. 'Don't let them near us, Papà!' he begged.

"Illuminato had a voice like thunder. 'Manton, you coward, shut your mouth!' he roared in front of everyone.

"I still remember the grateful look on Dom's mother's face, the shame on my father's. His shame became mine, too."

"But he was only trying to protect you," protested Leo. "It's so infectious, the pox, isn't it? I know *you'd* have been worried about me."

"Well, they laid the boy down on a bed. His head lolled back. His forehead burned like fire. Illuminato stood near, his back to the boy. I saw him close his eyes for a moment. The room was so still, as if even the bricks, the table and chairs were waiting until Illuminato took his next breath.

"Then he swung around and knelt down to the boy. Their faces were almost touching. He stared into Domenico's face and suddenly the air began to crackle between them. Illuminato's eyes glowed green as a cat's —sparks flew and the boy's face was lit by an incandescent gold, silver, oh it was like lightning, Leo, a flash of silver on a dark, hopeless night. The boy moaned and tossed on the bed. His mother watched, rocking, the tears dropping from her chin. But then, it must have only been seconds—and Domenico lay still. He gave a funny little smile and turned on his side, for all the world as if he was just falling asleep after a big dinner and a goodnight kiss.

"'He'll be well,' said Illuminato. He went back to the table and poured himself a cup of wine. 'Leave him there to sleep, signora. Come now and eat with us.'"

Leo gazed at his father. He'd never heard so much from him—about their family, about the past. He wanted to hear more, he'd sit there forever in that same spot and never move a muscle if Marco would just go on telling him these things, these secrets that *mattered.*

Marco stared into the fire. Leo sat still, hardly daring to breathe. He watched his father's profile, the eyes sunk in memory, the glow of the fire bathing his cheeks.

"Only once," Marco said into the silence, his voice still far away, "just once, did I get close to my grand-father. Close enough to feel his power on my skin."

"When was that?" Leo whispered gently. *Don't break the spell, gently now…*

"It was in the cave, his place of wizardry. You could feel him all around you there, in the rock, in the sandy floor; there was this taste, I don't know, a special heaviness in the air. He took me with him one day, just the two of us. Oh, Leo, it was so thrilling. Being with him was like standing on top of a cliff face, exhilarating but safe—he'd never let you fall. I stood close to him, I remember that my head came up to his waist. He had a silver girdle and a tinderbox tucked into it and I stood so close that I could breathe him in. I tried to breathe in his energy, the crackle of his power; he smelled of ashes and sparks. I thought if I could just fill my lungs with him, that heavy candle grease smell, I could touch the lights of his soul. But it didn't work. I saw his power,

I watched with wonder, but he never became a part of *me.*"

Marco wrenched his eyes from the fire and turned to Leo. "I couldn't give you that, son. I couldn't pass on a power like that because I failed."

"But you were only young. You said to me that it takes time, practice—"

"Yes, yes, but when it really counted, when I was a man, I failed."

"How? How did you fail?"

Marco shrugged. "I don't know. I didn't *want* to use magic—*dio,* I couldn't even save your mother ... But she lay there in her yellow cloak—"

"Who, Laura?"

"Yes, Laura, lying there in the cave in her yellow cloak. She looked at me with such trust...what could I do? I put a cushion under her head, she was mumbling, she was far away, but I had the heart of her—I *saw* her, I did. And I thought, if I gazed long enough, gathered her up in my vision, I could heal her, just like my grandfather did. I could transform all that was diseased, purify her..."

"So what happened? Did you lose concentration?"

Marco rubbed his hands over his eyes. "I don't know, son. I felt the shift start to happen, the slide of her soul towards me, and I had her there, all of her, in my mind. Who knows, maybe my heart was roaring too loud, but suddenly I couldn't hang onto her any more. I felt her curl away, she slipped like a stone from a peach, and escaped me. She had the energy of a wild one, a mad woman. The fever made her crazy and she leaped up. She was running and running and I couldn't catch her, I couldn't. And then the night swallowed her up and I never saw her again, even in my dreams."

Leo was quiet a moment, imagining. His father's face was white and gray in the shadowlight.

"But, Papà, did you see where Laura went? What direction she was headed?"

Marco sunk his head in his hands. "She was running towards the lake." His voice was low and shuddering. "There was a terrible mist that night, it clung to everything. A wind started up, it had a voice—roaring, thundering over the lake. Oh, son, how can I tell you the horror? The voice blocked out any other sound. Waves whipped wild, the spray and the mist...The last thing I saw was Laura at the water's edge. She looked back, it was just for a second, and then the dark reached out and took her."

Marco lifted his head. His face was ashen. He glanced away from Leo. "I won't ever speak of this again. What I will say is that my magic brought us disgrace and misery. Merilee's family will never forgive me for what happened—or you, for being my son."

"It's only Aunt Beatrice, Papà, she's the one full of venom. Merilee's told me how her mamma loved me like her own, she practically raised me—"

"I won't talk about it any more, Leo. We have to obey their wishes. Stay away from Merilee and the damn lake, do you hear me? Now go to bed and let me get on with my reading."

Leo hovered behind his father's chair. His mind was buzzing—thoughts whizzed around like a bunch of bees in a hive. He saw his father's pale face, the lines between his eyes deeply drawn. He saw the slight tremble of his mouth. But he couldn't stop. The buzz of questions in his head became one loud insistent voice, shouting over everything else.

"Papà," he began in a rush, "I heard it last night. Down at the lake. There was a voice, a ghostly call. It was awful, Papà, it made you want to go there, find it, smash it or save it... I felt as if it was calling me. But it scared me so I couldn't sleep. Don't you see, the only way we'll ever know is to go and seek it out ourselves—"

"Enough!" Marco cried, slamming down his note-book. "There are laws, and you must obey them."

Leo drew himself up. He lifted his chin and saw that he was almost as tall as Marco. He noticed the slump of his father's shoulders, the drag of skin hooding his eyes. And all in the same moment, Leo felt a piercing sadness and triumph at the strength coursing through his young heart.

"Papà," he said quietly, "I am a wizard with the twin signs and I've been practicing magic for six years now.

Why else did you spend all those hours teaching me, if not so that I could use my power?" With a sudden blaze of courage, he took hold of Marco's hands. "If I do see that witch, Papà, you can be sure I'll destroy her, I swear it on my mother's grave. And just think, there will be no more disgrace and misery. The Pericolo family will be heroes again, and we will all be set free!"

Leo's shining eyes stared into his father's face. But Marco Pericolo only looked at him sadly, as if Leo had just announced, like silly old Signor Butteri, that everything would be all right because he had just bought a whole stack of red furniture, enough to cure all the illness in the world, forever.

Chapter Five

Merilee woke early on Saturday morning. She curled her toes under the blankets and thought, *Leo*. Then she threw back the bedclothes and tiptoed out into the courtyard.

The air was cool and shiny, dew still sparkling on leaves and grass as if the morning were a bowl of crystal. Merilee hugged her nightgown around her and began to plan her day.

There were her jobs to do first, of course. She'd feed the hens and the pig. She'd sweep the floors and peel the vegetables for lunch. And then, afterwards, when Aunt Beatrice and her mother retired for their siesta, her time would be her own.

Merilee's heart lifted. A familiar feeling of excitement swept through her like a fresh breeze. But as she went back inside to get dressed, the trickle of anxiety that often came with the thought of Leo now became a steady stream. She remembered the smooth surface of the lake parting, heard that awful, breathy moan, and her heart began to thump.

She pulled on her boots and buttoned her dress. The devil take him, why did he always have to push and pull at things? Why couldn't he just let the world alone, and accept it as it was? She thought of his fierce face as he made his promise, and sighed. She knew that if *she'd* accepted things as they were three years ago, when her family forbade her to see Leo again, she wouldn't be planning her day with him now.

"And I wouldn't give him up for anything," she said to herself determinedly.

For lunch, Merilee and her mother prepared a delicious minestrone. They'd had to do battle with Aunt Beatrice, of course, who'd wanted to make the entire meal herself—with Merilee as kitchen maid, that is. "You'll only tire yourself, *amore*," Beatrice had nagged at Francesca. Still, they ate the soup with the thick crusty bread that Aunt Beatrice had baked that morning, and very good it was too, as they told her several times.

But Aunt Beatrice just waved her hand. "Oh, *si*, I had to get up before dawn this morning to bake that for you."

Francesca began to protest, murmuring how sorry she was, but Beatrice just charged on.

"Then it was just rush, rush, rush—there were ten aromatic posies to make up for the apothecary—he's always running short of things for his shop, he's the chaotic kind, you know, quite disorganized, I don't know how he runs a business. But he relies on me, so I couldn't disappoint him, could I? And I'd promised Signora Scardino that I'd make a new face salve for her—she's so particular, with her awful dry skin. Oh, I'm quite worn out. Still, if I didn't keep going, what would happen to this family, I ask you?"

The family had given up saying that they would be quite all right, thank you, as Aunt Beatrice always seemed to turn quite deaf when they did.

Merilee watched her aunt as she chewed. Large square chin, meaty hands always hovering like a sturdy pair of gloves over her mother's. Merilee tried not to show her irritation as Beatrice smiled falsely at her mother, offering her a tonic of lavender and myrrh, scolding her slightly, treating her as an invalid as she had done ever since Laura disappeared.

It seemed to Merilee that from the moment Francesca began to shrink with grief, her sister grew and bloomed with power. Merilee saw her studying their faces greedily as they ate, hungry for the praise that she was owed. She was forever busy, clattering cutlery, measuring and labeling herbs, smelling of wild and potent things. A whirlpool of energy surrounded her like a small cloud, powerful and noisy, and you kept far away unless you wanted to be dragged into her universe and enslaved.

Beatrice slept in Laura's room now, where the floor was strewn with aromatic herbs. Cloves, sage, and rosemary—Beatrice said they helped her remember her dear niece. Ever since Laura was very small, Beatrice had taught her about the healing properties of herbs. When she went for a walk in the forest, Laura would often bring a bundle of plants back with her and faithfully copy the stems and flowers into a book she kept under her pillow.

Merilee almost never visited the room these days. When she crunched that carpet of herbs underfoot, the pungent smell made her think of her sister's white face when she was ill. Merilee wanted to remember her as she'd been before that, but lately it was growing harder to recall her laugh, or the secrets they had shared.

After lunch, when the soup was gone and their "tonics" drunk, Aunt Beatrice saw Francesca to her room for the siesta. Before she retired herself, Beatrice turned to Merilee. "While we're resting," she told Merilee, "you could sort that rosemary and thyme you said you found in the forest. I'm getting a bit short of them both. I trust you at least know one from the other by now. Your sister used to sort and mark them for me when she was still in leading strings. Leave them in two packets on the dining table."

"Yes, Aunt," Merilee replied stonily, and went to her room.

She kicked the bedpost angrily. Oh, why hadn't she

remembered to pick the herbs? Now she'd have to collect them this afternoon, and get back early, before the old beetle woke up. Her time with Leo would be cut short, and there was so little of it, anyway.

"I should have given her the hemlock," she muttered, as she looked in her drawer for her cloth bag. But she felt soothed as she found her beautiful mahogany recorder and put it in the bag with her latest music score. Then she took off her sandals, swinging them from her fingers as she crept soundlessly out of her room, across the cool stone floor and out into the fresh afternoon.

Merilee ran through the fields that bordered the village. Cherry trees pink with blossom embroidered the hills and rows of grape vines wove straight as seams down towards the forest. *Run like the wind,* she told herself wildly, and suddenly she was filled with such freedom and happiness that she sang it out loud. Her long skirts swished round her ankles and she picked them up, feeling the grass scratch her bare legs and the wind whip against her.

Leo was waiting at their tree, by the path that led to the lake. Here the trees grew as close together as teeth in a comb, and the path was so overgrown with roots and pine needles that you would never have noticed it if you didn't know it was there.

"What a miracle!" Merilee laughed. "You, sir, are an

early Leo Pericolo. How did this happen? How can there be such huge and monumental changes in the universe? Just a minute and let me examine you—perhaps you are a changeling, a transformation!"

Leo grinned, and bowed deeply. "Oh, Miss Merilee, it is me, your Leo that shared your milk when we were babies. Look, I've still got the scar from when we spilt our blood."

Merilee frowned, the image of Aunt Beatrice and her shouting face suddenly looming at the front of her mind.

Leo, who knew her so well, grinned. "Ah, don't worry about old rat-face. Did you bring your recorder?"

Merilee nodded and drew it out of her bag.

"Let's have a song then. Have you made up anything new?"

"Yes, it's going quite well, I think. But it's hard to get the whole thing there in your head when you can only play in snatches. Aunt Beatrice hears even when I play under the bedclothes, and comes running in with a face like a beetroot."

"You know, I go crazy sometimes thinking of the stupid rules that woman makes in your house. I've never understood how she can lord it over everyone, even your father."

Merilee shrugged. "He says he just wants an easy life. It seems like Aunt Beatrice is the only one with any spark in our family—and she's got enough for ten. But it's curious, you know, even though she's so busy with her own concerns, she always seems to know exactly what other people in the house are doing. It's a bit scary."

The gift of the recorder had been the only agreeable event occurring after Laura's illness. A week after she'd disappeared, the young troubadour who'd danced with her knocked at the door. He held a recorder like the one his friend had played during that evening. "I'd like you to have it," he said to Merilee, pressing it into her hand. "It was the last time you saw her happy. The music will remind you of her dancing. You know, I'll never forget your sister."

Aunt Beatrice, who had come to the door at the same moment, smiled widely at the young man and told him how sorry she was that they were all too busy for him to come in. "Some other time when you are passing this way," she said, and firmly clanged the door shut in his face.

"I'll let you keep it," she told Merilee, "only on the condition that you never play it in this house. It will make your father and mother's grief worse, and I can't abide that silly recorder music anyway."

Leo settled himself on the leafy ground, his back resting comfortably against the tree. "Let's not think about them all for a while. They're enough to turn milk sour." He turned to Merilee. "Will you play your new song for me?"

Merilee took out a sheet of music.

The notes she blew were so high and pure, and the rhythm so lively that it shifted Leo's mood entirely. He suddenly felt like dancing. He tapped his knuckles on his knees, and let the music wind around him. Like a shimmering thread, it tied up all his thoughts and feelings, holding them tight, then releasing him, sending him tumbling into some new place that had no walls or fences, just endless fields of happiness. He could have listened to her forever, there in the forest, under the tree.

"*Magnifico!*" he cried when she finished. He clapped so hard his hands were crimson.

Merilee laughed with delight. When Leo looked at her like that, with such enthusiasm and admiration, she felt different, clever, *spectacular*—why, maybe she truly could do anything! She might travel the world with troubadours, play at court, compose new harmonies that no one had ever dreamt of before.

"Maybe one day soon I'll be good enough to earn my living this way," Merilee said. "And then we'll just run away, we'll escape like two birds out of a cage, and fly!"

"*Mamma mia*, Merilee," Leo grinned, "you're beginning to sound like me! Why don't you play another song and we'll pretend we're in Venice, in that grand Piazza San Marco, with all the gondolas gliding up and down the canals—"

56

"And the fat merchants in their silk robes strutting around the streets like pigeons—"

"Calling out, 'Who's that pretty musician in the square? I'll pay her 1000 lira for a song!'"

And so Merilee played on until the air amongst the thick trees grew cold and sunlight hardly passed through the leaves.

"Oh, Leo," Merilee groaned, when they both came back to the world of the forest and looked about them, "why do we always do this?"

"Because we never have enough time, that's why." Leo suddenly looked fierce again, like he had last Wednesday coming back from the lake, and Merilee's heart sank.

"I told Aunt Beatrice that I was late last time because I was looking for her wretched rosemary and thyme," Merilee said. "So now I'll have to go and pick some. Only I'm going to be late again."

Leo sprang up. "I'll help you. We'll do it together, it'll be quicker."

But just then, as Merilee was packing her recorder into her bag and Leo was putting on his hat, they both heard a noise. It sounded like a branch snapping, further up the path.

"Quiet!" hissed Leo. They both held their breath. Merilee's heart was pounding so hard she couldn't hear anything else.

A whiff of perfume, thick and spicy, drifted up. Merilee's stomach tightened. She smelled dried herbs, rosemary, marjoram. A feeling of dread so deep settled in her that her body felt bound to the earth, as if she'd grown roots and could never get up.

A thick-bodied woman in a long black dress strode out of the bushes.

"There you are, you sneaky little wasp!" Aunt Beatrice cried. She dived at Merilee, pulling her up by her long dark hair.

"Leave her alone!" cried Leo. He tried to catch hold of Merilee's hands, but Beatrice swung around to face Leo. Scarlet rose up into her face, coloring it completely the way a drop of paint colors a glass of water in a second.

"You devil!" she spat. "You dare to talk to me like that? What are you doing with my niece, sneaking around like the viper you are!"

"Aunt Beatrice," Merilee whispered. Her voice shook with shock. "We just happened to meet here in the forest. I was looking for more herbs, because the ones I collected the other day were not good, not—"

Beatrice let out a bark of laughter. Her mouth opened so wide that Leo and Merilee could see the great black gaps where her rotting teeth had been pulled. "More lies you're going to tell me? Come on then, give me some more rope to hang you with!"

Merilee was silent. Her legs trembled so much she was sure they'd just fold under her, and she'd sink to the ground like someone in a stupor.

"I knew you hadn't been looking for herbs, my girl," Aunt Beatrice hissed. "Since when have you ever interested yourself in my work? I ask you to learn the slightest thing about it, the slightest thing, and you sigh and tap your foot and the next day forget anything I said."

Glancing up at the crimson Beatrice, Merilee found it hard to remember how such a face had ever broken into a smile.

"So when you told me you were out late collecting herbs," Beatrice went on, "I wanted to laugh in your face. And sure enough, you left none on the table, and there was not a hint of them in your room."

Merilee looked down at the ground. She noticed a small brown cricket hop near the toe of her sandal. Aunt Beatrice is about to squash me, she thought, and I'm as helpless as that little insect. Only it can leap away and I can't.

"Oh, why don't you find someone else to bully!" Leo burst out. "What does it matter to you if Merilee has a little fun sometimes—"

"Fun?" Aunt Beatrice spat the word, like water hissing over hot coals. "You think she has fun with you, son of a murderer? What can you offer her—you, with your family of failures! You come from the loins of a drooling madman, from a demon whose name I won't speak, and you want to stand in the company of my Merilee?"

"Aunt!" cried Merilee. "Stop it!"

"What demon?" asked Leo. "Who?"

"You take her here, to the forest, down near the lake—you don't think about her safety, oh no, only your *fun.*" She bent down with a grunt and picked up the recorder left lying on the ground. "I heard this silly noise from the top of the forest. Enjoyed your concert, did you? Nice to be entertained."

Merilee stared at her recorder lying in Beatrice's plump hand. She thought of the sweat of her aunt's palm on the smooth wood, the smell of her heavy skin on the mouthpiece. "Please give that back to me," she said, trying to control the disgust in her voice. "It's mine."

Aunt Beatrice swung round to face her. "You can't be trusted, Merilee. You're a deceiving little liar, and liars don't deserve to own anything. You're going to be punished, my girl," and she grabbed Merilee's arm and began to pull her towards the path.

"She's not *your* girl, Signora," Leo cried after them. "It's not up to you to make the rules. You're not her mother!"

Beatrice stopped on the path. "How dare you speak to me like that, you vermin. I'll see that you're punished too—and *santo dio*, you'll wish you'd never been born."

"You can't touch me," Leo insisted. He was almost dancing with rage. "You've no right. Merilee's parents are the ones to decide her fate and mine."

Beatrice shook her head. "Ah yes, poor Francesca." She sighed, her face settling into mock-sad lines. "My sister, who's so wrung with grief she can hardly get up from her bed. You think she can make a decision about anything? Pah!"

As Leo glared at Beatrice, he slid without thinking into *seeing* her. It was as easy as diving into a pond. And there at the bottom, at the heart of her, sat a little girl. She was curled with her knees drawn up to her chest, her head lowered against them. As Leo looked further, he saw she was all closed up like a clam, except for her hands. Her arms drooped beside her, and her palms lay open, empty, like bowls waiting to be filled.

Leo felt a stirring of pity. She was the loneliest thing he had ever seen. But then Beatrice moved, giving Merilee a yank, and suddenly a shadow dropped over the little girl. She looked up and he glimpsed her face. A sickness rose at the back of his throat. The girl stared at him with snake eyes, yellow, flickering. Her green scales glittered and her forked tongue darted in and out of her mouth like a warning. She had a snake's head.

Leo closed his eyes.

"You're coming with me, my girl," Beatrice said as

Merilee struggled to pick up her sheet of music and push it into her bag. "We're going away for a while."

"Where?" cried Leo and Merilee together.

Merilee tried to hang onto Leo's glance, but Beatrice was pulling her up the path, through the thick-growing trees. He stumbled after them, their voices drifting up the hill away from him. He caught snatches of words, but his own terror was jumbling everything he heard.

"For how long?" Merilee asked. "How long will I be away?"

Leo heard no reply.

The last he saw of Merilee was her cloth bag, flapping open and empty against her shoulder as she ran.

Chapter Six

Leo crouched on the forest floor. He kept thinking about the bag. He couldn't think of anything else. As soon as Aunt Beatrice came into his mind, or Merilee's tear-wet face, he thought of the bag. The soft canvas, the black clasp undone, the way it had hung open, empty.

He began to run through the trees, back down to the path where they'd met. He had to find Merilee's song. It seemed so important suddenly that he could hardly see the bushes, dull and matted with dusk.

Leo arrived home just as his father was lighting the lamps. The room looked cozy and unusually tidy— papers stacked in orderly rows on the shelf, the stone floor swept, the table laid with a fine embroidered cloth. And there at the head of the table sat Signor Aldo Butteri.

He raised his glass of wine to Leo as he came in.

"*Buona sera,* Leo," he greeted him. "Come and sit beside me!"

Leo glanced over at the fire where his father was ladling pasta into three white bowls.

"Go, go," cried Marco happily, "go and sit. Look what our friend has brought. *Accidenti!*" Marco sucked his finger where he'd splashed a drop of boiling pasta.

"Porcini pasta, wine, guests," said Leo slowly. "This must be some kind of celebration."

"You could say that!" cried Marco as he brought over the bowls. He filled their glasses. "Tonight Signor Butteri has brought us a gift that holds the most important discovery in the world."

Signor Butteri gave a little cough, waving his hand a little as if to say "oh, it's nothing," but he was glowing with pleasure and pride, his face lit up like a ripe red pepperoni.

"Look!" Marco pointed to a book that lay open on the table.

"*Fabric of the Human Body,*" read Leo, "by Andreas Vesalius, 1543."

"Yes!" cried Marco. "Can you believe it? At last a book of human anatomy is published, and here we have it lying casually open on our own dining table! Hah! Look, Leo, drink it in, turn the pages, read, study, be amazed, but make sure your hands are clean first."

Leo looked. In the center of the title page there was

an illustration of Vesalius dissecting a corpse. Leo grimaced. His father's favorite subject.

He pulled a stool up to the table. There was nothing to do but sit and listen. Maybe he would think of something—something heroic and brilliant—while the talk washed over him.

"I was lucky enough to be present at a lecture Vesalius gave in Padua, last year," Marco said. "He was dissecting a forty-year-old male—dropped dead after choking on a turkey bone—and a hundred students were watching the operation. They couldn't believe their luck."

Aldo Butteri took a sip of wine. "I hope this book doesn't encourage your strange ideas, Marco. I only got it for you because you insist on this kind of thing, but I don't hold with the temple of the body being invaded by heathens, as you well know." He clicked his tongue in disgust. "It's quite against the law to use a human subject. Before this bold fellow Vesalius came along, dogs or pigs were good enough."

Marco gave a hoot of laughter. "Yes, and it was while watching pigs being slaughtered that the great Leonardo da Vinci discovered the heart is a mere muscle—"

"Preposterous nonsense!" cried Aldo, choking on his wine. "The heart is too noble—it's the center of the life force, you savage! The heart heats the blood, filling it with the glorious vital spirit!"

"You should attend one of Vesalius's lectures yourself, Aldo," Marco replied, grinning. "I'm sure he'd convert you." He turned to Leo. "Lecturers before him always got a barber to do the cutting, only pointing to organs with their nice clean wands. But with Vesalius you get the real thing!" Marco was rubbing his hands together, eyeing his friend cheekily. "He walks into the lecture room holding up a real kidney in his hand for everyone to see, or a liver, or a piece of stomach—"

"Ah, but the vital spirit isn't something you can *see*," Aldo pointed out solemnly. "Not like the stomach," and he patted the mound under his girdle.

"Well, *my* stomach is about to jump up through my mouth," Leo said, pretending to stick his fingers down his throat. "Can we talk about something else during dinner?"

Marco gave him a playful push. "Oh Leo, the stomach is the most extraordinary organ. And the intestines —see the large one?—it's so long that if you unraveled it, maybe you could wind it twice around the courtyard outside!"

Leo put his fork down.

While the two men ate and argued, Leo turned the pages. It *was* a startling book. Every first letter of the page was illustrated to show some stomach-churning activity of the body. He was looking at L, where a group of children were happily relieving themselves over the lower bar of the letter, when Marco leaned over and cried, "Aha! That's where all this good pasta is going to end up, isn't it!"

Leo rolled his eyes and the two men roared with laughter. Signor Butteri poured another glass of wine and Leo knew that soon Marco would be reminding him that he'd had enough for a man in his condition and Butteri would protest and they'd go on discussing the body and its problems until midnight.

Leo looked at his father's face, flushed with wine and excitement. He loved Marco's enthusiasm, but so often it meant he neither heard nor saw anything else. He was like a river rushing through its course, not stopping for anything, taking branches or trees or people with him as he tumbled towards his destination.

Marco would be no help.

Leo fingered the sheet of music he still had in his pocket. He thought of Merilee as she was dragged along through the forest. "Your family of failures," Beatrice had said to him. Leo winced.

"Indigestion?" asked Signor Butteri. "You should take an infusion of fennel. I got some yesterday from the apothecary—Signor Eco. Very soothing to the stomach, it was."

Leo sat up straighter. "Was Signora Beatrice there? I mean, when you went to see the apothecary?"

Signor Butteri chuckled. "No, but she might as well

have been. Old Eco was in a rage about her. 'Always bossing me around,' he told me, 'as if *I* worked for *her!*' She sounds like a fury, that one. Works hard, mind you, Eco said, and she has the knowledge of a Wise Woman, but sometimes he wonders if it's worth all the agony of having her around. Always fussing, shouting orders at him in front of customers, telling him off." Signor Butteri shuddered. "Couldn't stand it myself."

Marco got up suddenly and took the empty plates. His face was no longer vivid and happy. But two round spots of color still highlighted his thin cheeks.

"Still, when I saw him tonight," Butteri went on, "he was full of smiles. He'd just seen Beatrice—"

"When?" cut in Leo.

"Oh, a couple of hours ago, just before I came here. Anyway, he said she'd dropped in, in a great rush and dither as usual, to tell him she was going away. Imagine! Eco could hardly stop smiling!"

"Did she say where she was going?"

"Yes, now let's see if I can remember. It's in Tuscany—"

"Well, here is some fresh prosciutto and cheese," Marco said loudly, clattering down the plates in front of them. "The gorgonzola is particularly good."

"Fiesole—that's where it was. You know, the little town, not far from Florence."

"Mmm," Marco savored his cheese, "it's so strong

that it stings the back of your throat. Try some, Aldo!"

"Did she say why she was going there? Or for how long?"

"Mm, the gorgonzola's good," Signor Butteri said, loosening the cord around his waist, "but the parmigiano I had yesterday was better. Now let me see, Eco said she was going to some meeting of Wise Women, and he was glad to be rid of her for a while. He'd make up the aromatic posies himself now and—"

"Did she say how long she'd be away?"

"Well, not really, but he did say these meetings only happened every few years. They exchange recipes and potions and there's some kind of initiation ceremony for new candidates."

"New candidates?"

"Yes, girls who want to become trained in the art of herbal cures. Some of them stay on forever—they're the Wise Women of Fiesole, haven't you heard of them? Often they're the first to find a herbal medicine for some sickness or other, cures apothecaries take for granted now." Signor Butteri helped himself to some more cheese. "Take lavender, for instance," he went on, leaning back in his chair. "Excellent for back ache—using the essential oil, of course—and it eases my gout pain too, I can tell you. Of course *some* people, ignorant villagers, you know, think the Wise Women do the devil's work, mixing witch's potions and the like. Scared of them, they are. But that's all a lot of rubbish. You know how stories spread around here..."

Marco winked at Leo and slapped a huge piece of cheese onto his son's plate. "Eat up, boy!" he cried, but Leo noticed that he'd only had one small bite of his own.

Leo sat quietly, letting the men's talk float around him. He was trying to remember. The Women of Fiesole—he had a picture in his mind of a huge stone wall, of women behind it, quiet, studious, like nuns in a nunnery. Merilee's mother had once told him about it.

Anxiety filled Leo's body. The wall towered in his mind. How could he ever get her out of there? He couldn't imagine his Merilee cooped up like that, like a bird in a cage. What kind of a life was that? He felt alarm pinging through his body. Wildly, he wondered if Anxiety was there in that book, under A. Which organ would it affect? The heart? His was racing so hard he felt dizzy.

He wondered if Merilee was still at home. Was she packing? Could he catch her before she went? His stomach dropped. He saw Beatrice's face as she stood over him, mottled and angry like a hunk of salami. He saw the sly snake of a girl inside her. And he saw himself, puny as a mouse, squeaking at her feet.

He kicked the table leg. All those stupid fantasies he'd had—how one day he'd save Merilee from robbers, savage wolves, cutthroat pirates—and look, he couldn't even face up to her aunt.

"Family of failures" was right. Well, wasn't it?

He watched Marco talking, hunched over the book with his friend. His father might as well have been in another world, on Jupiter or Saturn, for all the help he gave.

Just then, Marco broke into a laugh. Leo's own lips twitched in sympathy. He felt something break inside him. He realized, suddenly, how much he loved his father's laugh. He thought how Marco had watched his wife die with her new baby in her arms, how he'd struggled as Laura fled from him, how he must have woken every day with fear of losing the people he loved, and still he could laugh. Get excited about things.

He was braver than that old salami-face, thought Leo. Braver than any of them.

And now, Leo decided, I'm going to try to be, too.

Leo stepped out into the night. He took a deep breath, filling his lungs. The air was sharp, cool for late spring. He began to walk quickly and quietly through the narrow lanes, keeping close to the buildings and their shadows, until he got out into the wider country, across town, to where Merilee lived.

It hadn't been hard to leave the house. Marco and Butteri were so deep in conversation that they'd hardly noticed when Leo excused himself and said he was going to get a breath of fresh air outside. "Take your cloak, it's still chilly at night," Marco reminded him, "and don't go beyond the courtyard." Then he'd turned back to his friend.

Leo was warming up already with the brisk walk. He began to jog as the spaces between the houses grew wider, and the grass became soft and springy under his feet. He was trying to make a plan as he went. But mainly he just couldn't sit still in that house any longer.

Somehow he'd get Francesca to listen to him. He'd explain about Beatrice, how false she was with that forked tongue of hers. He'd persuade her to defy Beatrice for once. Surely she'd do that for her own daughter!

He was close now. The sky was huge and black above him. The fields sprawled in darkness behind, the lamps in the windows of the houses pricking open the night like the eyes of small animals in the dark.

Maybe they'd escape, he and Merilee, he thought as he found the stony path to her cottage. They'd go to Venice and join a group of traveling troubadours. They'd just up and run, run cheering out of that house, away from Beatrice and her potions and her evil temper, and no one could catch them. They'd run until there was nothing but the sky and the earth and their whole lives in front of them, free.

As Leo came to the steps that led up to the door, he heard a clanging of wheels on the cobblestones and the sharp clop-hopping of hoofs as a carriage turned into the yard. He darted back into the shadows of the bushes, and waited.

The great ironbound door opened and Beatrice whirled down the steps. She carried packing cases, and a box filled with little jars and bottles. Slowly, reluctantly, Merilee followed.

The horses snorted as the driver tied the reins to the tree beside the house. "Good evening, Signora," he said. He nodded to Merilee. "Signorina."

Beatrice was handing over her packages to the driver, with strict instructions as to how they were to be stowed safely in the carriage without breakages, when Francesca came running down the stairs.

She flung herself on Merilee, hugging her tightly.

Merilee stood still as a stone. Her dark head rested in her mother's neck. She was like a hunted doe, thought Leo, some wild animal that has been caught and has given up.

Over her daughter's shoulder, Francesca cried, "Beatrice, look at her. She's too young to go—she's homesick already, aren't you, *cara?*"

Merilee said nothing. She just stayed where she was, with her face nestled in that warm, sweet-smelling valley of her mother's neck.

"I don't want her to go, Beatrice," Francesca said. Her voice was pleading, as if Beatrice were not her older sister, but rather her mother or the ruling queen of a court.

"Nonsense," spat Beatrice, getting rid of the last of her packages. "What Merilee needs is some discipline. She needs someone watching her all the time, someone who won't be too soft. I told you I found her with that devil-boy today. She deliberately flouted the rules, and you, my darling sister, are just not up to dealing with that kind of behavior."

"Beatrice, for heaven's sake, she's not a criminal—"

"No, Francesca, but she's spending time with something worse. Now please let her go and we'll be on our way."

Merilee's arms went around her mother. She gripped her hard.

Now, from the shadows of the path leading up to the house, there came a voice. "'Cesca, my love, where are you?"

A stumbling figure loomed up into the light.

"Papà!" whispered Merilee. She moved towards him.

"Franco," cried Francesca. "Thank goodness you're here. Tell her she can't take Merilee. She's too young to start that kind of life, she doesn't want it."

Franco waved a jug of wine in the air. "Ah, leave it alone, Francesca," he mumbled.

His words were slurred. If they'd been written on a blackboard, Leo thought, they'd look blurred as if all the letters had been rubbed together with a duster. Leo could smell the stink of wine on Franco's breath, as he burped loudly and lurched towards the carriage. He tripped on a loose stone and went sprawling over on the ground. The jug smashed and Franco let out a cry.

"Damn and blast," he swore. "I'm bleeding, 'Cesca. Oh, I'm going to be sick—help me!"

Beatrice stared down at him in disgust. She pointed at him with the toe of her shoe, as if he were a particularly ugly species of insect. "What kind of education will your daughter have here, Francesca? What kind of life can she lead with this *ubriaco*, this drunk for a father?"

"All right, all right," Francesca said tiredly.

Beatrice reached out and took Merilee's hand, pulling her towards the carriage.

Leo's heart was thumping. Now, I should do something *now*, he told himself. But he felt frozen, paralyzed. His legs wouldn't move. His throat was dry.

Merilee didn't look back at her mother or father as the driver helped her inside. Leo watched the darkness swallow the small pale moon of her face. Beatrice swung up into the carriage after her, and leaned over the side.

"*Arrivederci!*" she called merrily. "Stay well and get plenty of rest, Francesca, dear!"

"It will only be for two weeks, then, won't it?" Francesca called back. "I'll see you both in a fortnight, won't I?"

But the driver had already whipped the horses and the wheels began to spin and Beatrice was calling goodbye so loudly that Francesca never heard a reply.

When all the pieces of the broken jug had been picked up and Francesca had helped her husband inside, Leo came out of the shadows. He walked down the stony path, into the swim of darkness beyond it. He began to run, his feet fumbling over uneven ground. He ran blindly, trying to escape the hot spurt of shame that was flooding him.

A rabbit hole sent him tumbling and he lay where he fell, not moving. His arms and legs splayed out wide on the damp, cold grass. He felt like a fallen star, grounded, burned out, useless.

He closed his eyes and all he could see behind the lids was the word, *failure*.

Chapter Seven

It was two and a half weeks since Merilee had gone, and Leo had heard nothing. Every day he did the same things he usually did. He washed, ate, did his lessons, went to the market, but the life had gone out of it all. Sometimes, in the afternoons, he played tag or spun tops with other boys in the square. But deep inside, he felt there was nothing to look forward to, no warmth in the days. Just a dull gray dust over everything, with a nagging stab of worry behind it.

Then at the market one morning, he saw Francesca. She was buying some new season's pears. He went and stood next to her, breathing in her familiar scent. Rose and jasmine. It made sudden tears prick behind his eyes.

"Leo!" Francesca turned towards him and put her hands on his shoulders. "It's so good to see you—*dio*, how much you've grown!"

It was true. He was nearly as tall as she was. They both glanced nervously about as they began to wander through the stalls, talking.

Leo could hardly believe his luck. It just didn't seem real, as if they were walking in a dream. How different it all was without Beatrice hovering near. He kept expecting that any minute he'd wake up and Francesca would disappear, like mist in the morning.

"Have you heard from your sister?" he asked boldly. Francesca's face darkened.

"No. I haven't heard a word," she said. "Not one word. I don't know what she can be thinking of—she knows how I worry."

Leo's tongue burned with things he'd like to say. But he didn't say any of them. Why spoil this time with Francesca? He just wanted to keep on standing there, feeling safe with her, having her trust him.

"Will you let me know when you hear something?" Leo asked. "You could leave a message with Signor Butteri, or Signor Eco."

Francesca looked uneasy, fiddling with her necklace. Then her face cleared. "Yes, I will," she said suddenly. "I shall do what I like. I know how you care for Merilee."

"Thank you," said Leo, and without thinking, threw his arms around her waist. She hugged him back for just a moment.

"Oh, Signora, you forgot your pears," called the man

behind the fruit stall. Francesca turned, clutching her basket, and walked quickly away.

Leo stayed. He bought two pears. Her scent was still in his nostrils. He remembered her bending over him when he was little, her smooth fingers combing his hair after a bath. He remembered a story she told him about a little hen and a wolf. There'd been so many stories before their midday nap.

His throat ached and he began to walk too, away from the busy market and the hurt.

The meeting with Francesca changed Leo's days. He'd seen how her face softened and came alive when she looked at him. She'd hugged him close, her cheek pressed against his. For those few minutes at the market, Leo had felt himself loved. And it gave him faith in himself again.

Now when he practiced his magic, he concentrated with new energy. He was most himself when he was immersed in "seeing" something else. He felt he was using all his powers, flexing every part of his gift, and he was determined to get better. Be as good as he could be. As good as his father had hoped.

Failure, family of failures. When Beatrice's words floated into his mind, he tried to think of Francesca. He thought of Merilee and her songs, and all the games they'd ever played. And it gave him strength. He had the twin signs after all, and if he lived up to the power he was born with, then maybe he could rescue Merilee and send that Beatrice—and any other old witch—packing!

Some days he worked so hard that he missed the market, forgot to prepare dinner. He walked around with his head full of things he'd "seen." In his mind, he talked with them, fought with them—it was hard to let them go. Small nuggetty presences, they hulked inside him, clinging to his thoughts, refusing to be banished. He could never be alone any more—his brain rustled with creatures and shadows, the essence of things.

At night, Leo fell into bed exhausted. It was as if he'd run for hours, when all he'd done was sit still as a stone all day. He had to use all his energy to concentrate.

Only the voice still nagged at him. At night, when he was falling asleep, the breathy sound blew in through the shutters. *Leo, whoo, Leo soon!* And he'd turn over and hold the pillow over his ears.

Leo had no trouble "seeing." In fact, he sometimes thought he saw too much. It was the transformation part that was difficult. When he looked at a stone, an apple, he could see the heart of it so clearly—the rightness of the thing, the inevitability of it—and he was reluctant to change it. Often he'd become so convinced by the essence of something—all the glittering grains of sand in a stone, the messages inside a seed—that he couldn't touch it. He saw the meeting of ancient oceans and boiling earth—who was he to fool with that?

"You have to hold that thing in your mind, all of it, and then see the otherness of what it will become," Marco explained to him one night at dinner.

But Leo shook his head in exasperation. "It's like holding two sides of an argument in your head at the same time, and being equally convinced by both. You'd have to be strong for that—you'd need the heart of a lion!"

Marco looked at him curiously. "Are you afraid?"

Leo stared at his hands. "I don't know. Maybe."

Marco nodded.

Leo had often privately wondered if Marco had ever looked into *his*, Leo's, own heart. What would he see there? Once, when Leo asked him, Marco just said, "That is for you to discover." Whenever Leo felt afraid or weak, he feared what Marco had seen inside him. Was it a mouse, a poor shivering creature, and Marco didn't want to tell him?

"Sometimes," Leo said slowly, "a thing seems so right, just the way it is. What if I spoil it, what if I fail, and destroy it, so it's not one thing nor another? Then I'd know I wasn't a good wizard—I'd be a dunce!"

"How will you ever know if you don't try? To go to the second stage of transformation, you need to know all the details of the new object. In a way, you have to become the thing for a moment yourself, in order to understand it." Marco looked away then, and stared out at the fire. "That's where you can get lost. You must never lose your grip then."

Leo looked down at the table. His father was moving his empty glass around, making a wet circle on the wooden surface. In the silence, they could hear the rain starting. Leo knew his father was thinking of Laura. He didn't know what to do or say to make it better. Marco probably thought of Laura every single day.

The next morning, when Marco had gone to work, Leo set off early for the market. After he'd bought some fruit and cheese, he sat down for a moment, piling his packages beside him on the low stone wall of the piazza. The early sunlight was warm on his face, and he sat idly for a while, content to watch the passersby and listen to conversations going on at the stalls.

"*Ciao*, Leo," called Fabbio from his meat stall. "Why don't you take a few of these sausages home for your papà. You know how he loves them!" Fabbio was hanging great slabs of cured ham and salami onto the hooks of his stall.

Leo smiled and waved at Fabbio. It was true, Marco couldn't resist Fabbio's sausages—always fresh and spicy. But Leo just wanted to go on sitting there for a while. Lazy, he felt so lazy ... He'd get them later.

A customer walked up to the stall just then, so Fabbio

turned away to greet him. Leo watched them, grinning. Fabbio was the best salesman at the market. When he described the succulent qualities of his meat and just how to cook it, the juices started in your mouth. He'd wave his arms around, his endearing double chin wobbling with enthusiasm. No one ever left Fabbio's stall without a package.

But something was different about this exchange. Leo couldn't see any arms in the air, or hear any excited talk. The men's voices were low, intense—perhaps this was a friend of Fabbio's and they had some other business to discuss. Still, Leo felt uneasy.

He studied the customer. The man wore no hat or cloak, and his long hair was matted with straw. Just then, the man smiled and laughed at something Fabbio said, putting a friendly arm on his shoulder. Yes, the man must be a friend, Leo told himself.

Feeling restless now, he bundled his packages together and stood up. As he wandered a little nearer to the stall, he glanced sideways at the man. And that was all it took. Just a glance and Leo had him. He looked at the pale eyes of the man and saw straight through, into the dark soul inside.

Leo dropped everything he was holding and darted forward. He didn't stop to think what he was doing. As he leaped upon the man, he yelled, "Back, Fabbio!"

At the same instant, the man pulled out the dagger

that he'd had hidden inside his shabby vest, and lunged at Fabbio. The dagger glinted, for just a heartbeat, above Fabbio's shocked eyes before Leo knocked it out of the man's fist and crashed him to the ground.

People from all around the piazza ran towards them. Fabbio was screaming, "He tried to kill me! He was going to kill me!" The fruit vendor flung himself upon the man, sitting heavily on him, while someone else tied his hands together.

The dagger lay where it had fallen, on the pitted wood of Fabbio's bench.

Leo led Fabbio away, over to the wall where he'd been sitting.

"He was my friend since childhood," Fabbio was sobbing. "Pietro, he had a hard life, never had any luck. He went away to try his fortune and I heard he'd been sick—some fever of the brain. It left him crazy. But why did he try to kill me?"

Fabbio stared at Leo suddenly. "You saved my life," he said quietly, glancing over at the dagger. He shuddered. "How did you know, how could you tell what he was going to do? You were there before he'd even put his hand in his vest."

Leo looked away. He saw the people gathering around them now, talking avidly, pointing at them. He was shaking. He felt something rising up from his stomach, flowing into his chest. He swallowed—was he going to be sick? The feeling was so strange, so unfamiliar. But Leo could feel himself smiling. His mouth was stretching wider and wider, he couldn't help it, as Fabbio flung his arm around him and pulled him up. Pride, that must be the feeling. Bursting, exploding *pride*.

"How did he know? I saw it all—he got there just in time! Who would have thought it—Pietro and Fabbio were boys together." The talk was buzzing all around him, as versions of the story spread through the piazza. "He's got the second sight!" people told each other, staring at Leo with wonder.

Leo stood next to Fabbio, struggling with himself. He longed to tell them, describe the vision he'd had: the crazed creature, half man, half animal—the rage on its face telling him so vividly what was about to occur.

Yes! Leo wanted to shout, I am a wizard, with the twin signs. So was my great-grandfather. Look at me, I'm a hero like him!

But he knew he must not. He knew the penalty of practicing magic. *The Church fears magic...The consequences of being discovered could well be death*. In the village, it was only Meri who knew his secret, and she kept it like the grave. He only had to think for a moment about the horror that would show on Marco's face if he told, and the words died in his throat.

So when the villagers clapped Leo on the back and marveled and exclaimed, he answered them with murmurs of "luck" and "being in the right place." Fabbio wanted to give him a whole piglet that had been hanging up on a hook, but Leo said he'd have to hire a cart to take it home. So Fabbio just loaded him up with his best sausages, and the promise of a year's free supply.

Leo opened his front door with cries of "Bravo, Leo! What courage!" still ringing in his ears. As he threw down the sausages in the kitchen, he realized how hugely, overwhelmingly hungry he was.

"I'll cook the sausages and celebrate!" he told himself and he did a little dance to the kitchen. It was only later, while he was chewing and savoring the spicy meat, that the full impact of the morning flooded him.

He had trusted his magic, that's what he'd done. He hadn't agonized or doubted himself. He'd known, like he knew that he had ten fingers on his hands, that if he wanted to save Fabbio, he had to trust his vision. It was the only truth he knew.

When he finished his sausages, he sat for a while longer. In the silence, there was a sense of peace and stillness and he rested inside it, like a cat in a warm patch of sun. But even as he emptied his mind—no thoughts, no tensions—a moaning sound trickled in.

Leo tried to block it, clapping his hands over his ears, but like water running into crevices, it found a way in.

Leo stood up. He still glowed with the triumph of the morning. He had seen something important, had acted upon it. Great heavens, he'd only had to glance at the man to see inside. Just like—dare he say it?—the great Illuminato. Maybe he was ready. Maybe he, Leo Pericolo, could hear the witch calling because it was time.

Without even putting on his cloak, Leo walked out the door and headed for the forest.

As he ran down the path, the smell of pine leaves reminded him so sharply of Merilee. He almost expected her to jump out of the bushes and shout, "Here I am!" as she used to when they played hide and seek. He thought of the time they'd been together down at the lake, the time when he'd so unthinkingly challenged the witch. He winced now, wishing he'd done that alone.

Leo didn't want Merilee to suffer. He knew somehow that the witch was his. His alone.

And there was the voice in the breeze now, lifting, blowing back his hair. Calling to him. *Whoo pheye ...* He clenched his fists. Well, he was ready for her, wasn't he? If I see the witch, he thought, I'll bring her into the light. Maybe she'll disappear like mist in the sun, maybe she feeds on darkness and secrecy, like all evil...

The trees gave way to sandy ground and there, in ten steps, was the lake. Leo breathed out with a gasp. His own thoughts had been so loud in his head, bolstering him, giving him courage, that now the reality of where he was sent a bolt of fear shooting through him. He picked up a stone near his foot. He cradled it in his hand. It felt good; smooth and flat and oval. The voice was beating in the air, like a pulse, snuffing out his own. It was hard to think any more. He squared his shoulders, but the muscles beneath his skin felt suddenly puny. What was it he was going to do when he saw the witch? What had he thought? His mind went blank, he didn't know...

In panic, he swung back his arm and hurled the stone into the lake. It skipped three times, bounding in a wide arc between each point before settling into the depths. Leo watched, mesmerized, as the ripples around each point grew deeper, faster, joining up with the one in front until there was a long line of swirling water, churning towards the horizon.

As Leo gazed, the blue afternoon sky dulled above the lake, and the air darkened. Soon there was no horizon, no definition, as blackness fell like a curtain, out there, at the far edge of the lake. Leo was trembling on the sand, his knees hardly holding him. But he went on staring into the darkness in front of him, trying to see beyond it, through it, while he held fast to his memory of the bright afternoon. Behind him there was the forest, still dappled in sunlight. Before him was the blackening dome of the sky.

As he looked, the darkness seemed to move closer,

like an approaching storm. Leo felt it settle over him, the cold fog of it against his mouth. Then the dark was in his head, it had seeped in like floodwater and he suddenly knew what it would be like to drown in there, to thrash in the darkness, die in the lake. The voice was circling all around him, in tighter and faster circles, like the ripples, like a noose.

With a cry, Leo flung out his arms and kicked against the dark. His feet felt the solid ground, and gratefully he clung to it, digging into the gritty sand until his fingers stung. Then he turned and ran, clawing at his eyes as he stumbled over the shore, racing into the blue afternoon. The breath was aching in his chest, his throat was raw and still he ran like the wind, away from the darkness, away from the terror.

For just a moment, at the entrance to the forest, he swung around to face the lake.

Help me! screamed the voice—near, it seemed so near—*Illuminato!*

Chapter Eight

Merilee had often dreamt of riding in a carriage like a great lady. She'd gaze around her, watching the fields and trees rush by in a tumble of green.

But there was only the night outside. She saw nothing but the dark outline of hills, streaming like veils behind the mist. There was the driver's voice from the front, urging on the horses, the harsh bark of the whip. And pushed right up against her, taking up most of the seat with her heavy cloak and layers of petticoats and box of sachets was her hateful Aunt Beatrice.

The lump in Merilee's throat wouldn't go away.

"Are you hearing me, girl?" Aunt Beatrice poked her with a hard finger. "You'd better learn to listen, and change your lazy ways."

Merilee was thinking of her mother. The thin, heart-shaped face kept getting smaller in her mind, like someone shrinking in size as you got further and further away from them. She wanted her mother's face back into focus, big and real and comforting. But her mind wouldn't do it.

"If you keep on like that, looking all around like a great idiot while I'm talking to you, you'll be locked in your room as soon as we arrive."

The carriage bumped over the narrow road. Merilee swallowed hard. Her throat ached with tears. But she clamped her teeth together and wiped her eyes quickly with the back of her hand.

"How long is the journey?" she asked.

"Long enough for you to change your ways and show some respect," was the answer.

Merilee turned her head away. She hated breathing in the heavy flesh of Beatrice. If you breathed someone in, they became a part of you. She couldn't bear the thought of taking in air that had once settled in the dark caverns of Aunt Beatrice's body.

A tide of panic rose in her chest. She shifted in her seat and Aunt Beatrice's elbow shot into her side. "Sit still, fidget bones," she snapped.

Two weeks, Merilee told herself. I'll just have to hold my breath for two weeks, and then I'll be free. I'll breathe so deep I'll just float away, like a feather on the breeze.

"So please behave yourself," Aunt Beatrice was saying. "You'll be in the company of the most respected Wise Women in the country—my *friends!* It's very important to me that you work hard and do well. Your dear sister was a delight to teach. *She* was never rebellious or lazy. Try to be more like her. I beg your pardon?"

"Nothing, Aunt. I'm just—"

"At the last meeting," Aunt Beatrice looked at Merilee slyly, "there was a young girl who just lolled about brushing her hair all day. 'He loves me, he loves me not.' Oh, it was sickening. You know what they did to her? Cut off all those long golden curls and burned them in her room. Pah!" Beatrice gave a great shout of laughter. "What a stink!"

The carriage rolled on, parting great curtains of dark on its way north, to the town of Fiesole.

Merilee had fallen into a dream when the wheels finally stopped. She jolted awake and saw they'd come through a huge iron door, set in a wall that circled them like a stone arm. Beatrice paid the driver, who began to grumble, turning over the small coins in his hand.

"A flea couldn't live on that," he muttered.

Beatrice glared at him icily, and he fell silent. As she thrust packages and cases into Merilee's arms, the driver winked at Merilee.

Merilee smiled back.

"Get off with you, you insolent beast," Beatrice hissed at the man, "and be thankful you had the chance to accompany such honorable ladies."

Merilee saw him roll his eyes and spit into the dust, but he hoisted himself into his seat and took up the reins.

"*Buona sera,* signorina," he said just to Merilee, and in a second the carriage was gone.

"Fancy speaking to us like that," Beatrice said angrily, picking up her case. "You see, it's your fault, you with your common manners—you invited that peasant to flirt with you." She sniffed. "Comes from all your keeping company with that troublemaker back home. You only encourage bad behavior."

She sighed heavily, as if the weight of a hundred ignorant girls lay on her shoulders. But as she turned to look at the elegant garden that led up to the grand building before them, her face changed.

"There, young lady," she crowed, sweeping out her hand at the view, "I hope you are grateful for the opportunity of becoming a member of an Order such as this!"

Merilee stared. She dropped a box of little jars on the ground.

But Beatrice was so entranced by her surroundings she didn't even notice.

As they struggled up the path with all their packages, a servant in a coarse gray dress with a black cape came hurrying towards them.

"Greetings, ladies," said the woman. She pulled nervously at her servant's hat of linen tucked around her head.

Beatrice pushed her cases into the woman's arms. Merilee saw that the woman had a slight figure, which barely reached Aunt Beatrice's shoulder. Soon she was loaded up like a donkey. Beatrice wasn't finished yet. She thrust a final package under the woman's chin. The veins stood out on the servant's forearms.

"Aunt," Merilee said quickly, "I'll carry mine. Surely the signorina can't manage all of them," but Beatrice gave her a sharp dig in the ribs and told her to mind her tongue.

"The woman's a slave, for heaven's sake," she whispered. "That's her job. And a lot better off she is too than back in that freezing old Russia or Poland or wherever she came from, without a roof over her head or decent people to serve. Signorina indeed! Pah!"

Merilee walked silently behind them. She tried to wipe away the effect of Beatrice's words that always settled like scum over any still surface. She kept moving, staring straight ahead of her.

The Academy soared above them, a massive three stories high. Merilee had to crane her neck till she ached, to see to the top. But it was so beautifully proportioned, so simple with its regular arched windows and wheat-colored stone blocks, that Merilee felt calmer just looking at it. As they drew closer, she saw that the building was lit by an invention of iron lanterns. On thin stems the little flames leaned out from the corners of the building like sparkling flowers.

She followed Beatrice through the open door into an entrance hall. Her eyes swept up the marble staircase which led, the servant said, to the main living rooms upstairs.

"Some of the ladies are still dining," the woman told Beatrice. "If you would like to take some refreshment there, I'll put your things in your rooms."

Beatrice waved her hand at the woman as if she were batting away a fly, and marched ahead of her up the stairs.

"Thank you," whispered Merilee.

The place was truly wondrous, she thought. Never had she set foot in such a grand *palazzo* as this. The marble floor, the glowing tapestries on the walls ... The size of the entrance hall alone was staggering—you could fit several bedrooms in here, she decided, her eyes widening.

Merilee grinned suddenly, thinking of Leo. "What a waste," he'd say with disgust. She imagined his bustling energy as he set about with plans of housing poor families amongst all this generous space.

But when she came to the dining room, she couldn't help letting out a cry of admiration.

"The Green Room," Beatrice hissed in her ear. "Don't speak until you're spoken to."

The room was like a gleaming, well-kept garden. The long walls were covered in green silk, shimmering with leafy shadows cast by the fire in the hearth. A procession of candles stood straight and tall as trees along the wooden tables, strewn with plates and jars of white wine and fat bowls of fruit. Everywhere there were women sitting, standing in groups, huddled around on cushions talking. The hum of busy conversation and shouts of laughter filled Merilee with a sharp thrill of excitement.

A woman in a low-necked gown, embroidered with pearls, stepped out of the group near the fire.

"Welcome," she said. She walked towards them with a slow smile.

Beatrice rushed forward with her hands out. "It's absolutely wonderful to see you, Brigida!" she cried so loudly that several women nearby stopped talking and turned to see. "And you're looking magnificent—my, how smooth your skin appears—are you using my new face salve? You know, it's been such a success at home, I'm quite worn out with all my customers! Well, that and all the work I've had to do for the family. It's hard to keep it all going single-handed, I can tell you. This visit will seem quite a rest cure!"

Brigida just smiled and turned to Merilee. "Come here, young one, don't be shy. Let me introduce you to all the company."

Brigida only had to put up her hand and all the noise in the room stopped. "I want you to meet Merilee," she said, "the young niece of our busiest member, Beatrice Alberti."

The women clapped and as Merilee looked around and smiled and bobbed her head, she picked out one girl from the crowd who couldn't have been much older than she was. Or perhaps the girl was nearer Laura's age, she thought—if Laura had still been alive.

Merilee felt shy and lost in that huge sea of strangers.

But the girl gave Merilee a grin, friendly, intimate, as if they'd known secret things about each other for years. She patted the cushion next to her invitingly.

Merilee hoped no one took that spot before all the introductions were made. Beatrice had started on a long speech about a new potion for curing inflammation of the lungs. Merilee found her mind wandering off down little lanes of thought, like a puppy who'd been let off its leash.

But when Beatrice drew breath, Brigida said something that pulled Merilee up sharply.

"So young Merilee is our new Initiate into the Order of Wise Women." Brigida was smiling at her. "She will be receiving the usual instruction in the mysteries of our Art, and I'd like you all to join me in wishing her every success in her new life."

The women stood. Each one held up two fingers in a V sign, entwining the forefinger with that of the woman beside her. The V became W, and Merilee saw the room filling with the sign of the Order, fingers fluttering like birds high above her head, flying up and down until the last, seventh time the fingers came to rest, pointing straight at her.

"*Salute* and *fortuna!*" the women cried together, until the air echoed and shivered with their high rich voices.

Merilee tried to smile. Beatrice grabbed her hand to perform the ritual, placing her meaty finger over Merilee's. She hoisted Merilee's hand high in the air as the women had done and Merilee suddenly saw herself, not in the beautiful Green Room glowing with silk but in her yard at home, where Beatrice had made her stand, all those years ago, with her hands up high to drain away the poison from Leo's blood.

"A new life," Brigida had said. The words rang in Merilee's ears. It sounded much more than two weeks. It sounded like a sentence—the sentence of a lifetime.

She looked at Beatrice's face, scarlet with triumph.

In that moment, Merilee understood she was her aunt's creature now, as surely as if Beatrice had put a chain around her neck and a bone at her feet.

The next morning, Merilee woke in a soft, wide four-poster bed. She sat up and looked about her. A finely carved chest of drawers sat opposite, with her clothes neatly stacked inside. There was a chair and a writing desk, with a fresh quill and ink pot, and next to it was a small fireplace.

It was perfect. Merilee smoothed the crisp white sheets over her legs. The edges were embroidered with tiny roses. Merilee couldn't have dreamt of a more lovely room. But it chilled her just the same.

Last night, it had been hard to see anything much when she came to bed. The slave woman (whose name was Consuela, she told Merilee, and she came from Spain, not Russia) brought her upstairs with a candle. But Merilee had been so exhausted that she'd collapsed on the bed in all her clothes, and fallen fast asleep.

There had been so much to eat—great glistening trays of roast lamb and rice cooked with almonds and slabs of cheese, but Merilee had to sit at a table with Aunt Beatrice so she hardly tasted a thing. Beatrice talked—or shouted—over everyone, telling her latest news of pills and potions, of the "helpless" apothecary she continued to rescue (who, heaven only knew, must be *beside* himself with worry at being without her now). When someone at the table began to speak, Beatrice pounced on them like a cat with a mouse, and they never even got a syllable out before she'd crunched it up and swallowed the bones.

Merilee sat writhing in her chair, torn between trying to distance herself from this embarrassing relative of hers, and fighting an unbearable need to run away. How *could* a person have so little interest in anything outside of herself? How did her aunt ever learn anything when she never listened? Perhaps in this place, you just had to absorb the atmosphere through your skin, like sunlight on bare arms. Whatever it was, Merilee hoped it was something simple like that, because she found it very hard to concentrate at all.

There must have been thirty women in the dining hall, but Merilee discovered that there were sixty-five in all. The woman called Maria who sat next to Merilee had been yawning and wriggling in her chair, and soon she whispered that she was off to find her friend.

"Where are the rest of the women?" asked Merilee.

"Oh, some have retired to their rooms to study," replied Maria, "and others like to meet with special friends in their apartments. I wouldn't mind joining them, actually," she added, lowering her voice. "There's a good game of cards going on in Sandra's room, I know for a fact."

Merilee grinned. Aunt Beatrice disapproved of cards —said it was gambling, the devil's vice.

But at that moment Beatrice swung around and scowled at Merilee.

"I suppose you know so much you don't have to listen to how one makes up a pomade?"

Maria excused herself just then, saying she had a headache. But she had to wait for another ten minutes while Beatrice gave her advice on how to treat it.

Watching her go, Merilee decided fiercely she might

just learn how to play cards. Or maybe there was a music group who liked to sing or play recorder in the evenings. And Beatrice could go and jump in that lake full of foul and dreadful things and drown herself!

But next to being back home, Merilee wished most of all that she could go and sit on the nice comfortable cushion next to that smiling girl.

The girl knew something, Merilee was sure. That smile was welcoming and friendly, but it was knowing, too. And Merilee needed all the information she could get.

Merilee lay in bed for a while thinking of the night before. Scenes streamed past in her head, faces she'd like to know better leaped out at her. It was all so different, so colorful and *big* somehow, after living all her life in one small village. But clouding everything was Aunt Beatrice, lurking over her shoulder like a giant shadow.

From along the corridor somewhere she heard a gong sounding. "Breakfast," she thought, and jumped out of bed. Last night, with all the worry and surprises, she'd hardly eaten a thing. Now she was hungry and the new day had given her hope.

She took a fine linen undergown from the drawer and chose a red dress to slip over it. A new girdle her mother had packed, of white silk webbing with silver threads, was tied around her waist. She gave her long hair ten brush strokes (her mother had always done a hundred), then dashed out into the hall.

She could hear laughter, and around the corner she met Maria and three others who were all hurrying to the "Yellow Room" for breakfast.

As she entered, an ocean of voices crashed around her ears. It seemed that all the women were present, sitting at six long tables. The pale yellow silk of the walls reminded her of eggs and cheese and her stomach rumbled. She quickly glanced around, searching for the friendly girl of last night, when she felt two heavy hands on her shoulders.

"This way, young lady," boomed Aunt Beatrice, her breath stale in Merilee's ear. "Come with me." She steered her to the third table where Brigida was seated.

"We can't start too early with her lessons!" Aunt Beatrice said importantly, making sure Brigida heard.

Brigida smiled at no one in particular, and went on eating her fruit. Merilee was beginning to recognize that smile. It seemed kindly and a little vague, but you could tell that behind it Brigida was watching everything like a hawk and she'd make her own steely mind up, thank you, and there wouldn't be a thing you could do about it.

Merilee looked away uneasily and helped herself to some figs.

"First thing this morning, you go to Workshop 4,"

Beatrice told her. "You will be learning about essential oils—how we gather them, why we use them."

"Will you be teaching me?" asked Merilee, choking a little on her fig.

"Close your mouth when you're eating," barked Beatrice. "Unfortunately not. I have to give a lesson myself, on my Tonics." Her voice rose suddenly and she leaned forward on her elbows, towards Brigida. "I think the lecture will prove very interesting—I'm going to discuss the use of geranium and ginger, oils which restore vitality to the body with remarkable speed."

Brigida thoughtfully swallowed her egg.

Beatrice sat back on her chair sharply and turned to Merilee. "Listen to all that is said in your lesson, and take notes. I want everyone to see what a studious niece I have." She picked up a hunk of cheese and swallowed it. "Tonight I'll come to hear what you've learned. So pay attention."

Chapter Nine

It was late afternoon when Leo arrived home from the lake. He had wandered in the forest for a while, trying to quieten himself before he met his father. But Marco was already at the table, preparing supper, when Leo stepped through the doorway.

"Chop some more wood, will you?" Marco called as he looked up. "I'm bone-cold, there's ice in my veins."

Leo nodded quickly and went round to the courtyard where the logs were stacked. He was glad to be alone, his breath still ragged, his heart wild.

He dragged out a log and picked up the ax.

The hour he'd spent walking had done nothing to calm him.

Coward! he hissed as he swung the blade. *Dunce!* he spat, splitting the wood. *Call yourself a wizard?* For a moment, the dark rose again before his eyes, the impossibility of it, and despair made him crack the log in two, sending splinters flying.

"I can't even *see* now," he told the earth as he flung himself down. "A cat could see better in the dark than me. What have I against the weapons of witches?"

Leo split all the logs that were piled in the courtyard. He went on working for longer than necessary, beating out his frustration as he crashed through the wood. It was dusk when he finally threw down the ax and brought the night's logs inside.

"What have you been doing?" demanded Marco as Leo trudged inside. "I've called you twenty times."

Leo put the logs next to the fire and went back to close the door. Outside, there was the moon, not yet full, pearling a patch of sky.

As Leo leaned against the door, gazing out at the night, he asked himself a question. What if the moon had been full, down there by the lake? What then?

Leo sat at the table to eat with his father. There was a plate of fruit and cheese, and a pitcher of wine.

Marco gestured at the food and shrugged. "I saw that you bought sausages, but they'll keep for tomorrow. I'm not so hungry tonight—"

Leo stared at him. "But Fabbio chose them for you specially. They're your favorite kind."

Marco shook his head. "You got enough for thirty people—what possessed you to buy so many?"

Leo looked down at his plate.

"Fabbio gave them to me—as a gift."

He expected his father to exclaim at this, and inter-rogate him. Fabbio was a good friend but a shrewd merchant, and he didn't often give his best meat away for nothing. But Marco just nodded vaguely.

Leo watched him. He was relieved that he didn't have to explain about the day, make conversation. But he wondered at Marco's lack of curiosity.

Marco picked a pear from the plate and began to peel it. Leo noticed that his hands were trembling slightly, and his palms were sweaty.

"Are you feeling all right, Papà?" he asked. "Are you still cold? It's really quite a mild night."

"Yes, yes," said Marco. "I'm just a bit tired. I don't think that fish I had at the city market was too good today, that's all."

Leo cleared away the dishes. He helped his father out of his tunic and straightened the sheets on his bed. It was only early evening, and here was Marco getting into bed. Leo couldn't remember that ever happening before.

The afternoon's danger receded to a dull ache in his mind as Leo looked at his father. Alarm filled him. He went to close the shutters.

He'll probably leap out of bed in the morning, hungry as a horse, Leo told himself. But Leo took a long time to get to sleep that night. As he lay listening for the sound of Marco's breathing, the moan from the forest blew in, pulling at him each time he closed his eyes.

Leo was dreaming of his father standing at the edge of the lake, calling to someone, when a noise woke him. He sat up straight, his heart hammering. "Papà?"

"Leo, get me a bucket, quick."

Leo threw the sheets off and went to fetch it. He could hear the rasping of his father's throat, the raw scraping sound of a heaving stomach. He put a hand on his father's shoulder. Marco shook it off as he bent over the bucket again.

Leo sat on his bed, hugging his knees. He put his fingers in his ears. It was so scary, that sound. Scarier, even, than the voice from the lake. Marco shouldn't be sick—he was never sick. His shoulder had been damp with sweat. Leo had felt it through his nightshirt.

God, please don't let him be sick. Make him better now, please. He's all there is in the world. Please, oh please.

When Marco lay back on his bed, Leo took the bucket and sloshed it outside. He got a cloth and dipped it in the basin of water they kept for washing. Marco groaned. The sheets were wet beneath him. Leo felt his forehead. It was burning.

"Here, Papà," he whispered, trying to stop his voice shaking. He laid the cool damp cloth on his father's forehead. In a minute it was warm.

Marco suddenly sat up and leaned over the bucket again. The dry coughing, the shuddering for breath. Leo sat by, not touching him, holding the blue cloth.

The morning light shone in through the high window, making a square of gold on the wooden table. It drew a line across Leo's wrist, warming his head that lay resting on his arms.

He stirred and blinked at the light. Then the sinking feeling in his stomach returned as he remembered. He got up and crept over to his father's bed. Marco was sleeping now, but his breathing was heavy and he moaned a little as Leo wiped his lips and forehead with the cloth.

"Is it all my fault?" Leo whispered, bending over his father. Dread clutched at his stomach. All my stupid fault, he thought. Why did I have to go to the lake—hurl those insults, throw the stone? "Leave it alone!" his father had told him. "You don't know what you're dealing with."

He pictured himself at the market that day, full of silly pride. How he'd danced round the kitchen, certain he could do anything. But he'd always been like this, hadn't he—getting carried away, not thinking. Why did he have to go against the order of things, disobey his father? Leo banged his fist against his knee. *This* is what happened when you did that. This terrible thing. This punishment.

Leo stood up. He couldn't bear it. If he could go back in time and snatch away his words, his silly dare, he'd give anything. Even his power. Marco had known his own limits. Why hadn't *he?*

Leo had lit the lamp during the night and prised open Marco's box of papers. He'd looked under F for Fever in *Fabric of the Human Body.* But he'd found nothing. In Marco's notebooks there were a mountain of sketches and notes about bones and infected wounds and torn muscles, but nothing helpful to him. Towards dawn, he discovered another notebook—it had been at the bottom of the pile—and the papers were tied together with a special ribbon.

"The fever is the most vital element to cure. To reduce fever try tepid bath with infusion of Bergamot and Lavender. If necessary force her to drink water. She can't swallow. Her throat is too sore—she says there are needles in her throat. What to do? Cloves? She's crying, oh my love, don't cry, she won't stop crying. What should I do do DO..."

The writing grew big and black on the page and the rest was covered by an ink spot. After that, there was just his mother's name scrawled all over the pages—Rosa, Rosa.

Leo had found it hard to read any more because the pages kept blurring.

With the morning light, Leo got up from the mess of papers on the table. He shuffled them into some sort of order, then filled the cooking pot with water. While it was heating, he washed his face and dressed in his long hose and tunic. All these things he did silently, hoping not to wake his father.

As he moved about the house, his father's handwriting was always just behind his eyes. He could hear the scream in the words, the loneliness. *"What should I do?"* It was no wonder that his father spent his life trying to understand the human body. His magic had failed him: perhaps the answers lay in this new knowledge of medicine. Leo had only been six months old when his mother died. He hadn't been able to help. But now he was older. Old enough to get help.

Before he left the house, Leo soaked towels and rags in cool water, and sponged his father's body again. Marco woke briefly and smiled at his son.

"Papà," said Leo, feeling heartened by the smile, "I'm just going out for a short while. You rest, and I'll be back soon with some medicine."

But Marco had fallen asleep again, the smile still lifting a corner of his mouth.

Signor Eco, the apothecary, was at the back of the shop making a supply of lavender bags. Leo had to walk past the long bench at the front, lined with little bottles of oils and aromatic waters, and shelves fragrant with bouquets of herbs. The shop smelled busy and rich with all its complicated ingredients, and Leo's spirits lifted.

"Firstly, I'd burn rosemary and thyme in the room, to

110

prevent further infection," Signor Eco advised when Leo had told him the story. "I'll make you up a sachet right away."

The apothecary was reaching for neatly labeled bottles of herbs, bustling around as he talked. He had a large belly and big plump fingers and it always surprised Leo to see him handling the little jars and spoons and sachets so delicately.

"What about the vomiting?" asked Leo. "It didn't stop all night."

Signor Eco frowned. Leo had described very serious symptoms, and although he didn't want to show it, he was worried. He almost wished Beatrice was here.

"Look, Leo," he began, "we'll try these methods but we can also get some special advice. I have to go to Fiesole tomorrow—"

"Where the Wise Women are—"

"That's right. I need some more chamomile, the German kind, and Beatrice was able to get some for me. I told her I'd pick it up tomorrow, so I can ask her at the same time what her Order would do for a fever. You know, this chamomile could be good—"

Leo gave a little jump of excitement. He never thought he'd be so happy to hear Beatrice's name. The advice of a whole company of Wise Women! But then he stopped. "Signor Eco, don't tell her who the advice is for, if you don't mind. She's not particularly fond of my father—she might prescribe deadly nightshade or something!"

Signor Eco gave a hoot of laughter and his chins wobbled. "She may be a bossy bit of work, but she's not evil, Leo. I won't be back for a few days though, I'm afraid. I've got appointments all over Tuscany."

"All right, I understand. But when you go," Leo picked nervously at a scab on his thumb, "well, could you take a message for me to Merilee?"

Signor Eco scratched his belly. "I don't think Beatrice would like that. Aren't you two supposed to be—"

"Merilee would want to know about my father, signor," Leo cut in, looking wounded.

"All right, *va bene*," Signor Eco sighed. "But if Beatrice ever finds out, I'll be a dead man."

"She's not evil, though, is she, signor?" Leo asked him innocently.

Signor Eco snorted. But he gave him an ink pot and a quill and carried on making up the herbs for Marco. Hastily, Leo scratched a note to Merilee.

Dear You, he wrote, *When are you coming home? Are you a prisoner? I miss you all the time. My father is very ill with fever. Is there anything you can suggest? Write and tell me if you want to escape. Or maybe you've become so Wise you don't want to talk with the Unwise. Beware of Beatrice, Merilee. She's a snake—she speaks with a forked tongue. Don't believe what she tells you.*

L.

Leo blew on the ink to help it dry, then folded the letter into a tiny square. "There," he said, putting it into the apothecary's hand. "You won't forget it, will you?"

Signor Eco winked at him. "I'll put it with my money. I never forget that!" He handed Leo the packets of herbs and wished him luck. "I may be able to get a message to you sooner. Otherwise, I'll visit when I return."

Leo thanked him heartily, and almost skipped out of the shop.

As he walked home, he felt the sun like a warm hand on the back of his neck. The rain had cleared, leaving the streets shiny clean. Just writing to Merilee made him miss her less. It was almost like talking to her. There was just a gap in time until he had her reply.

But when he opened the door to his house and found his father lying on the floor, drenched in sweat, a cold terror swept any other thought from his mind.

Chapter Ten

Merilee only found Workshop 4 by accident. Beatrice had hurried off—"Heavens, is that the time!"—without giving Merilee the slightest clue where she was to go, and the room emptied as suddenly as if it were tipped up like a jar of rice and turned on its head.

Merilee found herself alone at the table. At the far end of the room was Consuela, stacking plates for washing. She was helped by two other servants who seemed to be arguing with her. Merilee felt silly sitting all alone like a stranded sheep, and stumbled outside.

She walked along a corridor until she came to another spacious room. The door was ajar, just barely open, but through it wafted a perfume of rose and jasmine so overpowering that tears started in her eyes. It seemed that just behind the door, so close, her mother must be waiting.

Shyly, she pushed the door open. She put her head in. There was no one.

She sat down on a low wooden bench. Shelves above her were crammed with jars of herbs and little pottery vessels filled with fragrance. Merilee let the aroma drift over her. She could have almost fallen asleep. But her mind kept flicking over to that strange, tiered structure in the corner of the room.

She'd never seen anything like it. Glass sheets were stacked one on top of the other in wooden frames. When she looked closely she saw that the glass was covered with some kind of greasy substance, and sprinkled over it were fresh petals. Merilee bent to take a great sniff.

Suddenly, behind her, she heard a footstep. She swung around and found herself face to face with the friendly young girl of the night before.

Merilee laughed with relief.

The girl was wearing a red silk headdress that sat, heart-shaped, above her forehead. Deep navy blue eyes smiled at Merilee.

"The aroma of love, wouldn't you say?" The girl nodded at the wooden structure next to Merilee. "What does that perfume make you think of?"

"My mother," said Merilee quickly.

"My Alessandro," said the girl. She stood next to Merilee and breathed in deeply. "I met him on the day I made my first pomade—from this very same contraption, you know."

Merilee was about to say no, she didn't know, and

how did this greasy business they were bending over end up as a perfume? And where were the usual introductions, and was this girl a student too, and what was her name? But she didn't get a chance.

"I wore the pomade in my hair, and he said I smelled like a rose from the garden of paradise."

"Excuse me," Merilee began cautiously, "but are you here for Essential Oils?"

"Yes, I'm your teacher—Isabella Innamorata at your service. At least that's what I call myself."

"So it's just us two?"

Isabella smiled at her, nodding. "Tell me, niece of the great Beatrice, who will come bursting in here like gunshot any minute to see what I *haven't* taught you—" They both looked up then as a clatter of feet passed the door and stopped, a long shadow snaking through the gap, along the floor. "Tell me, do you know anything about the essential oils?"

"Well, I—"

The feet went on their way and both girls grinned.

"Of course, *love* is an essential oil, if you want my opinion."

"But excuse me, *is* this Workshop 4, where I'm supposed to be?"

Isabella laughed. "Workshop 4? Yes, my sweet, here you'll learn how we extract the finest quality essences from our most delicate plants."

"But how does it work—I mean, with this 'contraption'?"

Isabella raised her eyebrows in surprise. "The glass is coated with lard, and the essence of these flowers is absorbed into the fat."

Merilee picked up a petal and sniffed it closely. "Is the pomade made from this?"

"Yes, from the perfumed fat—"

"And the essential oil?"

"Merilee darling, where have you been all your life? Separating the essential oil from the fat is one of the first experiments our students attempt at the Academy." She looked at Merilee closely. "Don't you know anything, sweetness? Aren't you the niece of Beatrice the Burrweed?"

"Burrweed?"

"Of course, *I'm* far more interested in Love Potions than medicines, I have to admit. Try a drop or two of sandalwood or rose and your young man will want to carry you away on a tide of romance!" She gave a noisy sigh.

"*I'd* like to be carried away in a carriage all the way home, actually," Merilee confided impulsively. She looked down at the floor. She hoped she hadn't been rude, but then Isabella was so, well, unusual, so frank, and the habit was catching.

Isabella didn't seem to notice. "Once you've been in

love, you'll know what I mean. In a couple of years, you'll be asking for my recipes—Evergreen Love Potion, by the way, is one of my best. Do you have someone special at home, then?"

"Oh, well, he's really just my best friend. Leo—"

"*Si, si,* there was talk of him last year. Dangerous type, they said."

"Dangerous?"

Isabella waved a hand. "That's only a description from our dear Beatrice. I didn't put too much faith in it, don't you worry. No, perhaps 'adventurous' is a better word for the young man, wouldn't you say? That's the word I'd use for Alessandro."

Merilee sighed. She knew she was going to hear a lot of other words about Alessandro, and she wished she could get back to the topic that really interested her.

"Courageous, defiant—except with his father—recklessly handsome. You should see his eyes! Mind you, there have been others—the boy who used to deliver the lard—ah, he was delicious, sweet as a peach. But then they found me and another girl making eyes at him, and they stopped him coming."

"They?"

"Her, you know, Burrweed and her allies. Still, maybe it was for the best because I do love Alessandro del Sarto, and I always will—even if they won't let me marry him."

Isabella's voice dropped mysteriously at this last

announcement, and Merilee could hear the girl willing her to ask more.

"Why can't you marry him—does he love you?"

Isabella smiled. "Yes," she said simply. "But his father happens to be a duke—so of course, I'm not good enough for his precious son."

Merilee felt her face grow hot. "And why not?"

Isabella walked over to the shelves on the wall. She picked out a small pile of petals wrapped in paper. Laying them carefully over the glass, she said, "I'm an orphan, Merilee. I have no family, no title or name except the one I've chosen, and no dowry to give to any man. What a lowly creature I am, *cara*—all I have in the world is my heart!" and she flung the last petals at Merilee, laughing at herself. But as Merilee bent to catch the flowers, she saw Isabella's eyes.

"So you've lived here always, since you were a baby?"

"Always. At least, as far back as I can remember. The women found me in the cathedral of Fiesole and raised me here. I'm very grateful, of course." Isabella sighed.

Merilee understood. She knew what it was like to be grateful, and trapped.

A light breeze stole in from the window behind them. It was cool and refreshing, and Merilee lifted her hair off her neck to feel it.

"*Che bello!*" Isabella breathed, turning her face to the window. "It's so warm in here, I could just melt." She began to fiddle with her hair, and when she took her hands away, long blonde curls fell to the floor, together with the padded ring of the headdress that had been holding them there.

Merilee gazed at the hair on the floor. There was so much of it. Then she looked back at Isabella.

She seemed like a different person. Her hair was cropped close to her head, jagged, short, like fur. With her big eyes and slim neck she could have been a young doe, caught in the forest. Merilee thought with a stab that she looked so young—vulnerable, like someone's lost little brother.

Isabella saw Merilee staring, and a blush spread over her bare neck. But she ran her fingers through her fur and said defiantly, "Of course, Alessandro hasn't seen me like this."

She took a step forward and took hold of Merilee's hand. "You can touch it if you want."

Merilee passed her fingers through the springy hair. "It feels like fresh-cut grass!"

Isabella grinned. Then she said softly, "Do you think he'll still love me?"

"But why did you do it?" Merilee burst out.

"Me? Do you think *I* would? My hair was my greatest asset! Alessandro used to say the alchemists would be after me, trying to spin it into gold. Down to my bottom, it was," she finished proudly.

But Merilee had stopped listening. Something her aunt had said, something on the way to Fiesole..."*You're the one,*" she whispered.

"The one and only! Meet Isabella the Disgraced. The female Samson."

"But how—"

"It was like this," Isabella said darkly. "One afternoon, around sunset, I met Alessandro in the woods by the olive grove." She glanced quickly at Merilee. "We often did—we aren't allowed to even see each other, so where else can we go?"

"I know all about that," Merilee agreed. "Go on."

"Well, we were sitting, talking. Actually, Alessandro was telling me how he couldn't live without me, when we heard someone coming towards us. We scampered away, crouching through the undergrowth. When I sneaked back home, so relieved at not getting caught, I didn't notice all the twigs and burrs in my hair."

"Oh, no!" Merilee clapped her hand over her mouth.

"Oh, yes," said Isabella grimly. "First thing at supper, Beatrice eyes me as if I were a criminal robbing her purse. Then she leads me out of the room by my ear."

"*Santo dio*, Beatrice the Burrweed!"

"She knew I'd been somewhere I shouldn't, and one of her spies had seen Alessandro leaving the forest. "That hair of yours is full of burrs," she spat at me. "We can't get them out, so we're going to cut it off. Maybe that'll teach you to behave like a lady!" I think she was afraid I'd infect the other women, the *new* girls—love's so contagious, you know, and *distracting!* She always said I was a bad seed. 'Heaven only knows where that one sprang from!' she says, shaking her head."

Merilee grabbed hold of Isabella's hand. A flame of anger was building in her belly. *"Dio,* how I hate her—I'm so sorry, Isabella."

"It's not your fault, Merilee. You can't choose your relatives! I could tell as soon as I laid eyes on you that you couldn't stand her. You were sort of shrinking away, leaning as far from her as you could without moving your feet. You looked like an essential oil, my sweet, separating as fast as you could from the fat!"

Merilee burst out laughing. But the anger was still making swirls of red in her head, so that she was laughing and groaning at the same time.

"The woman's a menace," she muttered.

"A hag from hell," whispered Isabella. She was dancing around the room, still holding Merilee's hands. "A goblin-faced pus ball, a toenail dipped in hemlock—"

"You sound just like Leo!" cried Merilee breathlessly as they swung around the room.

"He's a 'demon in human shape,' isn't he? A rascally reptile, a viper in the bosom of the family—"

Merilee stopped dancing. "Who said that? Beatrice?"

Isabella nodded. "She really detests your Leo, you

know. I'd watch out, if I were you, or you might lose your hair, too."

"But how did you hear about Leo?"

"Oh, I've got big ears—see?" She waggled them at Merilee. "You can see them now I'm naked. I listen to the gossip, that's all. Well, what else is there to do? This is like my family here, for want of a real one."

"But do you know why she hates him so much?"

Isabella stopped dancing. "Wasn't there something with your sister...his father..."

Merilee waved her hand impatiently. "Yes, yes, but I've never believed that's all it was. Everyone knew, including Beatrice, that Leo's father tried to do everything he could. He's a *good* man."

Isabella shrugged. "I've heard other things, strange things. There was some old argument, a crime committed, way back before you were even born. A crime of passion, perhaps...something that left the family cursed. But it's all ancient history, Merilee. Nothing you can do about it now."

Merilee's heart was thumping. "You mean someone in Leo's family—Manton, perhaps—did something bad?"

Isabella looked at her. For the first time, her gaze was uncertain, shadowed, as if she were hiding something. "I don't remember names very well, *cara*. But 'Manton' isn't familiar. It was an unusual name, something to do with light. But see how long ago?

Everything's forgotten. Leave it alone. History can't be remade."

"But—"

Both girls heard footsteps tacking over the stone floor outside. Isabella put her finger to her lips. The steps grew louder and sharper as they neared the door. But Merilee felt a sense of urgency building in her chest. Isabella knew something. This might be her last chance to hear it.

"Now," said Isabella in a loud voice, "what we've got to think about is the future, my girl. And if you're going to be a proper apprentice to that aunt of yours, I'd better get on with imparting my wisdom."

"Apprentice?" Cold dread settled like ice in Merilee's stomach.

Isabella raised her eyebrows. "Isn't she grooming you for that? Did you know that Brigida is leaving next year?"

Seeing Merilee's face, Isabella frowned and put a hand on her shoulder. Her voice softened. "Well, it's better that you know it now, sweet one." Isabella drew a deep breath. "Beatrice is hoping for the position of Head Wise Woman. She's determined to get it. I know for a fact that she wants to drag herself out of that backwater of a village you come from—sorry, her words, not mine. She wants people bowing and scraping to her. Only she needs a young woman to be her apprentice—all Heads have that requirement. You know, they have to pass their wisdom on to someone in training. Well, Laura, of course, was her first choice, being the eldest and all. Beatrice was teaching her—until Laura fell sick. Between you and me, Merilee, sometimes I think that's *why* she got sick."

Merilee heard a shuffle of feet along the corridor. A crowd of footsteps and a low buzz of talk streamed in through the door. Lessons must be over. There was no time. Merilee felt breathless, as if she were swinging high on a rope, and down below was the black scary sea of her future. She wanted to climb up onto safe solid ground, where she would know what was happening to her.

"So," she tugged at Isabella's arm as the girl swept around tidying the shelves, "how can I learn everything in two weeks? Because that's when I'm going home. Beatrice promised. She said it to my mother."

Isabella stopped tidying and looked into Merilee's face. Her navy blue gaze was direct and true. "To become an apprentice," Isabella said crisply, "a girl has to study here for one year. Beatrice has no intention of your leaving so soon, I'm afraid."

There was a clatter outside the door as if someone had dropped a tray. Isabella took Merilee's hand and began to walk towards the door. "But we'll be able to see each other, Merilee," she said in a lighter voice. "Often! We'll have picnics in the forest, midnight feasts in our rooms. Cheer up, you've still got me!"

Merilee didn't hear the kind words or notice the friendly hand in hers. She only felt the ice spreading through her body up into her heart. Trapped, that's what she was, as helpless as a rabbit in a snare.

Chapter Eleven

Leo unlocked the big, iron-studded door of his home, and trudged inside. His arms ached from carrying heavy packages all the way from the market. He dropped his shopping onto the wooden table and flung himself down in a chair. For just a moment he closed his eyes, concentrating on the light, free feeling in his arms. Then he let them fall by his side, the ache easing.

Leo went to early market every morning now. His father seemed to sleep best then, and Leo could get on with making the meals for the day. He looked over at the pile of food on the table. Eggs, cheese, rice—Fabbio had even run after him with half a peacock, because his father was ill. Leo's eyes burned for a moment. He'd never tasted peacock in his whole life. Marco said it was such a delicacy, only dukes or bishops—maybe the Pope himself!—had it for dinner.

Leo sprang up and began sorting the food to store in

the pantry. It wasn't good to sit still for too long because then he could hear his thoughts, and he didn't like them. After he'd put away the food, he'd go in and see his father. In just a minute.

During this last week, Leo looked forward to out-ings—even the market—more than anything. While he was out, he imagined that just for an hour or two, some kind of miracle might occur and when he returned his father would be sitting at the wooden table, happily exclaiming over a new notebook of Leonardo, or devouring a bunch of grapes. "I feel so much better!" Leo could hear him say.

On the way home, Leo would daydream, hope and dread jostling in his chest. When he neared the alley that led into his street, he had to count his steps or say Latin verbs to stop the feelings rising into his throat.

Leo pulled the curtain back and knelt down on his father's bed. Still asleep. He put his hand on Marco's forehead. It was hot and damp, but not as bad as yesterday. Marco had burned to the touch, and cried, talking gibberish. Leo had tried to soothe him, but Marco didn't seem to even see him. Leo just sat there on the bed. Those nights were dreadful, and Leo's own eyes were on fire with lack of sleep.

The nights were the worst. When Marco was feverish and Leo couldn't sleep, the moaning came. It trickled in from the dark outside, rising like poison from the depths of the lake. *Whooo, pheye*, it sang through the window. *Whooo, pheye*, it groaned through the walls.

Leo couldn't escape the voice. Even when he bolted the doors and windows, it whispered to him. Sometimes, when he was sure it said his name, he'd spring upright in bed, straining his ears, listening, listening. Sometimes it sounded as if it were right outside the door.

Now he wondered if the voice hadn't already got in, inside his own head.

No one else seemed to notice it. No one talked of it—at the market, in the piazza. Wasn't it growing louder, more demanding? But it was only Leo, in all the world, who could hear it.

Merilee had heard it once, too. He remembered her face, the thudding of their hearts. *Dio*, how he missed her.

Last night, the moon had been almost round. There was only a slight dent on one side, as if someone had cut a strip away. Tomorrow it would be full.

Leo looked at his father's sleeping face. The long proud nose, the fine cheekbones. Marco's face was so thin that the bones jutting under the skin were sharp. In five days, Marco had only sipped some soup and water mixed with wine. Leo could see the stripes of his ribs as he breathed.

In five days, Leo thought miserably, he had done no wizardry. He didn't have the heart. He couldn't

129

concentrate on a silly old stick, or an apple, or even a bird. What was the use? He felt his power weak and watery inside him. It was as if his vision had blunted, dissolved in fear. If he couldn't help his father with his power—and he was too afraid to try—then what use was it at all?

Must burn some more rosemary and thyme, thought Leo, getting up from the bed. Stupid just sitting here doing nothing. Signor Eco had said to fill the room with it continuously, to purify the air. Then it would be time to make the soup.

As Leo poured rice into boiling water, he wondered for the hundredth time if Merilee had received his letter. Would she have read it eagerly, taken notice of his warning about Beatrice? Would she be worried about his father? In his gloomiest moments, Leo imagined her scanning the words hurriedly, then stuffing his note into the folds of her dress, hurrying off to the next banquet.

Leo stirred the rice for a moment. Surely Signor Eco would be back today. He dropped the spoon with a clang on the stone floor, spraying water onto his legs. Damn it! Better not to think at all, he muttered to himself, he was such a dunce at everything lately. He took the peacock meat out from its wrapping and began to chop it carefully. The meat would add nourishment to the soup, and be easy for his father to eat. Then he'd peel the turnips and add a cup of wine, good for building up the blood.

Leo grinned suddenly, thinking of Signor Butteri's

enthusiasm for wine. "Liquid from heaven!" Aldo Butteri would cry, thumping his fist on the table. "Improves the blood, hastens digestion, calms the intellect, and expels wind. What more could you ask from a drink?"

Marco, who liked a drop of wine too, always chortled agreeably with him. But Marco was even fonder of a good argument, especially with his friend Aldo. "It makes fools of men, that's what it does," Marco would reply and Aldo would bluster and protest, "Only if drunk to excess!" growing redder in the face as he poured yet another glass of wine to "calm his intellect."

Leo plopped three turnips into the pot and set the soup to cook slowly. He was just sweeping the kitchen floor when a loud knock on the door startled him.

Aldo Butteri came every morning to see how Marco was progressing. Often he'd bring something helpful— daily, in the piazza, there seemed to be gossip about a new miracle cure. Yesterday, he'd brought scorpion oil. Four sips were supposed to flush out disease by causing excessive urine. A passing peddler had told Giovanni about it, who'd told Aldo. Leo had thanked him and tossed it out in the courtyard. He could just imagine, if Marco had all his wits about him, what he would say to his friend about *scorpion* oil!

"Have you actually seen someone swallow it, Aldo? Do you want to kill me? Ach—such old fables! Dangerous stories! Must you believe everything you hear? Let me give you a piece of advice, my friend: follow the example of Leonardo, and study the world with your own eyes. You'll stay alive that way!"

As Leo went to open the door, he thought of the witch in the lake, and the moaning. He'd heard *that* with his own ears, seen the parting of the lake with his own eyes. It was no story. But who had a cure for that? Marco wouldn't even talk of it. Sometimes Leo wondered if it was the moaning that kept Marco feverish at night.

"Buon giorno, giovanotto!" boomed Signor Butteri, tumbling into the room. Leo winced, hoping his father wouldn't wake. The morning siestas seemed to be healing for him.

"Good morning," Leo replied quietly. "Can I help you with that?"

Aldo was struggling with a huge red bath. Inside were two cushions of the same startling color.

"I thought I'd bring you this—yes, I know you have a basin, but it's tiny and it leaks and it isn't red. Where shall we put it down? Here, near the kitchen? The cushions are to put under your poor father's head."

"Thank you, Signor Butteri." Leo hesitated. "Would you like to see him?"

"Yes, my boy, I would. How's he been?"

"A little better today, I think. Last night, he was burning up with fever, but now he's sleeping. The fever seems to have passed—for the moment, at least."

"Good, good. Well, I saw Signor Eco this morning, and he was asking after your papà, of course, and he told me that a bath in tepid water will help reduce fever. Particularly if you add a cleansing oil such as juniper."

Leo stopped suddenly. "You saw Signor Eco? Has he returned?"

Aldo nodded. "Yes, just got back this morning." He searched in the leather bag at his waist. "Here, he gave me a bottle of juniper oil that the Wise Women made up. He said to put it in your father's bath. It will help expel infection and act as a tonic as well."

"Thank you." Leo put the bottle on the table. "Did he mention that there was anything else for me?"

Aldo looked puzzled. "Something? Not that I remember."

Leo couldn't help the gulp of disappointment rising from his throat.

"He was in a terrible hurry, actually," Signor Butteri went on. "He'd just come back from Fiesole, you know, and was due within the hour at Montepiano, to see a lady with infected toes." Butteri wrinkled his nose. "Pus. There are so many theories these days on how to treat it. I told him the old remedy my grandfather swore by— you cut a splinter from a door which a eunuch has passed through, and stroke the infected area with it three times, with three fingers of the left hand." Butteri sniffed. "Eco didn't seem much interested, though. Hardly stopped to listen. Still, he *was* in a tearing hurry."

Leo turned to lead Aldo to his father's bed.

"Oh, Leo," Aldo tugged at his arm. "I forgot—what with all the worry about your father. Eco did say he would be back by six o'clock this evening, if you wanted to drop by. He had something to tell you."

Aldo eyed Leo curiously. "A medicine, perhaps? A new herbal recipe?"

"Oh, yes, I imagine so," Leo replied quickly. How different you can feel from one moment to the next, he thought. "Come through and see how the patient is faring."

Leo led Aldo to Marco's bed. Aldo sat down heavily, and took one of Marco's hands. "Thin as a twig, isn't he?" he whispered loudly. "Leo, go and get those red cushions."

As Leo bent to pick up a cushion, he wondered how he was going to wait until six o'clock. So much of his life was about waiting. Waiting for his father to get better (please God!), waiting till Saturdays to see Merilee, waiting for her return. *Merilee!*

When Leo came back, Aldo gently lifted Marco's head and slid the cushion underneath. Marco opened his eyes for a second and smiled at his friend. It was a weak smile, but it was one of recognition and calm.

"There!" exclaimed Aldo.

"Ssh!" warned Leo. But he was grinning.

"That bit of red is already doing him good," Aldo patted the cushion with excitement. "The fever's in his head, you see. Your papà thinks too much, that's his trouble. I'm always telling him so, but will he listen? Red is the color of health and vitality. Nothing like it!"

Leo got up from the bed and silently beckoned Aldo to follow him. Reluctantly, Aldo left Marco and his red cushion, and strode over to the bathtub.

"Is that why you painted it red?" Leo asked, running a finger along the rim.

Aldo frowned. "Yes, that's right. Only painted the outside, though, because I wasn't convinced the paint would stay on when mixed with water. Do you think it will have the same effect, though?" he asked anxiously. "I mean, with the red not exactly touching the body?"

"It'll be fine, I'm sure," Leo said. "And I'll give Marco a glass of red wine to sip while he's bathing. That way he'll have red outside as well as inside. What could be healthier?"

Aldo glanced at Leo sharply. But Leo kept a straight face, busying himself with the soup.

"Good, good, excellent!" Signor Butteri exclaimed, encouraged. "Do you know, you *could* give him the wine in a church bell. Has much more effect than an ordinary old cup, I'm told, and drives out the fiends. You'll need to say seven masses, though, while he drinks it, so don't let the bath water get too cold. Well, my boy, I'll leave you to get on with your cooking."

When Signor Butteri had bustled out, still telling Leo about his sore legs and how busy he was, what with the orders piling up at the workshop without Marco, Leo closed the door and leaned for a moment against the cool wood. He let the silence in, watching the dust motes settle in the sunlight. Then he went to collapse on his bed. Just for a minute.

Half an hour ago, when he'd heard there was "information" from Signor Eco, he'd felt his heart thump, wild with anticipation. But as he lay there, his hands behind his head, an utter weariness came over him. "Something to tell you"—what did that mean? Was Merilee safe, happy? Maybe she'd sent back some advice for his father's treatment. Maybe she was doing well at her studies. But she wasn't here with him now. She hadn't packed her bags and come rushing home. She was far away—lost to him for almost a month, maybe forever.

Leo looked over at the red bath. People like Butteri were kind. Neighbors, shopkeepers, everyone asked how his father was each day, whether he'd like a nice bunch of raisins, a chat, some advice? But then they'd all go away. They'd take their comfort, the warmth of their voices and hands, and go home.

Leo felt his eyes burning. He laid an arm across them. Why did the people he loved always go away? His mother, Merilee, Francesca. It was terrible, the silence between him and his father. Leo was so used to all the words in the house, the arguments, the late-burning lamp, the discoveries. Now there was only the quiet of his father. The outside of him. Please come back, Leo whispered.

He sat up. The soup will be cooked by now, he thought. He would take it off the fire in just a moment and let it cool for when his father woke up. Then he'd fill the bath. Tepid water *was* good for fever, he knew. It said so in Marco's journal. He remembered Francesca giving him and Merilee those coolish sponge baths when they were little. Hot and irritable, their skin sore, the water would slide over their limbs, soothing the hurt.

Afterwards, Francesca would lie down on her bed, the two children on either side of her, their heads tucked like baby birds under her arms. Sometimes she'd sing them to sleep. Leo was gathered up, all of him folded like a present into her warm safe body.

Leo's face was wet. The burning became tears that trickled down the sides of his face into his hair. All the thoughts, the bad thoughts, came flying in. He let them come, beating their wings, crying at him with their shrill voices until his mind was dark and he sobbed, great hacking sobs of loneliness that seemed to come from somewhere deep in his heart, although he knew that it was only a muscle like any other because he'd seen it copied beautifully in his father's notebook.

He must have fallen asleep because when he woke Marco was calling and there was a smell of burning. He sprang up, alarm shooting through his body, not knowing whether to run to his father first or take the soup off the fire.

"Just a second," he cried and in one leap he was at the fire, seeing his precious peacock meat and nourishing liquid just a dried-out mess in the bottom of the pot.

"*Mamma mia, che cretino!*" he cried.

"Leo!"

Marco was half-sitting up in bed. He held out his hand to his son. "Could I have a cup of water?"

"Do you feel better?"

Marco nodded. "A little."

"Later I'll give you a bath, and then I'll add some water to the soup. It'll be all right, maybe, if I just—" Leo hopped up to fetch the water.

He watched his father drink it. Marco winced as he swallowed. His throat must be so dry and sore, thought Leo. What do you give for sore throats? He twisted his hands together. And how could he ever lift his father into the bath by himself? Wouldn't he need help?

Marco fell back on the sheets. He was asleep again.

The silence deepened in Leo's ears. He watched his father go away, back to the other world where he was alone.

Leo picked up the cup and refilled it with water. He

set it down on the little table next to Marco's bed. Then he went to wash his face and change his tunic. He would go and see Francesca. He couldn't think of anything else to do.

"Leo!" Francesca opened the door, startled.

"I'm sorry," he said quickly, "I didn't mean to disturb you, only—" He suddenly felt breathless, and put a hand on the door to hold himself up.

"Come in," said Francesca, glancing up and down the path before she closed the door behind him.

"*Caro*, you look ill." She took the hat from his head and smoothed the damp hair from his forehead. "You go up, you know the way, and I'll fetch some wine and sweetmeats. Go upstairs and catch your breath."

Leo climbed the stairs into the sitting room. He sat in the deep velvet chair. Everything was so familiar. The same richly colored murals, the portraits standing above the mantelpiece.

He looked first, as always, at the portrait of Caterina, Francesca's grandmother. It was startling how she looked straight out at you from the painting. Her heart-shaped face was Francesca's, but something about the eyes—the defiance in them—were her own. His eyes slid over the scar on her right cheek. It was more of a pit, really, a deep hollow left by the smallpox. Strange, thought Leo, how that feature in anyone else would have been disfiguring. It would be the first thing you'd see, defining the face, ruining any chance of beauty. But Caterina's splendor shone out, like a tide of laughter over one small protest. The glow of her eyes, the tilt of her chin seemed to come from some inner fire, some magnificence of soul.

She must have been loved, Leo thought. A beauty like hers would have commanded a whole troop of admirers. He thought about Merilee, and how much he missed her. It was hard to imagine people who lived so long ago feeling like he did. Then a thought struck him for the first time. Caterina must have been alive at the same time as Marco's grandfather, Illuminato. If they'd lived in the same village, they must surely have met. What would they have felt about each other, Leo wondered, still gazing at the painting. Illuminato was a great wizard, a miraculous healer—would Caterina have admired his power? And what about him—wouldn't he have seen the fire in *her*? Leo had heard different stories about what had become of Caterina; did the plague take her? Leo sat up. Perhaps there was a link between her disappearance and Illuminato, he thought suddenly. Maybe they'd once loved each other, just like he and Merilee...

Leo shifted restlessly in his chair. Next to Caterina were the portraits of Merilee and Laura when they were infants. There used to be a portrait of Leo, too, painted when he was four, but Beatrice had burned it after Laura died.

Leo closed his eyes. He could see everything better

that way. Each object in the room was alive for him. Every chair and cupboard had a silent memory wrapped inside it.

"That's good, you rest now," said Francesca as she came in with a tray. Sitting down near him, she poured white wine into his glass, adding water from the jug. "Try these sugared oranges, they used to be your favorites."

When Leo had drunk some wine and eaten, Francesca asked him about his father.

"He still has the fever," Leo replied. "But he doesn't bring up his food any more and today he seems better. Calmer."

"I've wanted to visit," Francesca told him, "I know how hard it must be for you. All alone." She looked away for a moment, reddening.

Leo cleared his throat. "I don't know what to do. How to help him properly, I mean. And I miss Merilee." His throat closed over.

Maybe he really only had a little mouse inside him, he thought miserably—just a scared baby mouse wanting its mother. Maybe that's what his father had seen, and would never tell him.

Francesca leaned near and took hold of his hands. She smelled of rosewater.

"It's just, why do we all have to be so alone?" he mumbled into her shoulder. "As if we were enemies, or strangers. Why does it have to be like this?"

"Beatrice—"

Leo flung up his head. "I'm so sick of thinking about her. Everyone doing what she wants, obeying her as if she were a queen or something!"

Francesca sighed. "Some people are stronger than others, Leo. They have more vital spirit in them—"

"I can tell you what Beatrice has inside her," Leo said in a new voice. It was harsh and knowing. "On the day she took Merilee away, I *saw* her."

Francesca waited, looking at him.

"I saw the snake coiled inside her."

Francesca drew in her breath. But Leo, still holding her hand, told her everything he'd seen. He chose his words carefully, picking them as if he were cutting out something very precious with the fine point of a knife. He had to make her see. He told her of the lonely little girl, so empty and sad, and how the girl's face had changed when a shadow dropped over her.

Francesca withdrew her hand. "I am the shadow," she said dully.

Leo stared at her. "You! How? You're warm and sweet, like the sun!"

Francesca shook her head. "For you, perhaps. But for Beatrice—well, I think I stole her light. When we were young, just girls in our father's house, I was pretty and people were fond of me. I had lots of friends. It came easily to me. I liked to dance and sing, I played the recorder well—" Francesca looked down at her feet. "I played so well that our father used to hold concerts in the sitting room, and all our friends would come to listen. I remember how Beatrice would glower over there," Francesca pointed to a chair near the sideboard, "her face dark as a storm. Sometimes she'd put her fingers in her ears for the entire concert."

"So," said Leo slowly, "she was jealous of you."

"Yes," said Francesca. "She was always heavy and awkward with people, didn't know how to converse, how to make the best of herself. She always seemed to say too much, or nothing at all. It's strange, she never learned how to listen to other people, you know, show an interest in them. And then, when I, the younger sister, got married before she'd even had an offer, well, you can imagine. She told me she hated me, wished me dead." Francesca took a sip of wine. "I remember her face at my wedding, it was frightening."

Leo was silent a moment, picturing it all.

"So now she's enjoying herself," he said finally, "lording it over you and your family."

"Well," Francesca lowered her voice, "this *is* her house. Papà was worried for her, you know, seeing she never married. He wanted to make sure she'd always have a roof over her head."

"But your husband—"

"Oh, Franco," Francesca motioned with her head

towards her husband's room. "You know what he's like. He lost all his family's money gambling. We had nothing. And now, since we lost Laura, the wine has become his only comfort."

Francesca and Leo sat in silence together.

Leo finished the sweetmeats and looked at the portraits on the wall. Merilee and Laura were sharing a smile, a secret perhaps, their eyes crinkling at each other in recognition. It was a very fine portrait.

Francesca followed his gaze. "*My* girls were always close, thank heaven." She smoothed her skirt over her lap.

Leo sat rigid in his chair. He felt confused and angry and overwhelmingly disappointed. Francesca's situation was difficult, desperate even, he understood that, but why—Leo felt guilty even thinking it. But in God's name, why couldn't she be *stronger*?

"What are you going to do about Merilee?" he blurted. "Beatrice might be planning to keep her there, in that fortress at Fiesole forever!"

"Oh, Leo, it's not a fortress, I'm sure—"

"Have you ever been there? It might as well be, anyway, if Beatrice is in command."

Francesca's cheeks grew pink. Her hand went to her lips. "Don't ask me to go against Beatrice, *caro*. I've told you all this so you'd understand. I'd be frightened, Leo. And all those Wise Women... oh no, it's too much. Let's wait and see—I'm sure she'll be back soon."

Leo watched as Francesca covered her face in her hands. She began to cry, and the tears seeped out between her fingers. Leo suddenly saw how much things had changed, that it was he, Leo, who had to be the strong one now, and he straightened his back in the chair as he made up his mind.

"Do something for me, then," he said, standing up. "Come and help me look after my father. He needs a cooling bath, and I can't lift him alone. The sooner he's better, please God, the quicker I can attend to Merilee."

Francesca leaped up in alarm. "Oh, Leo, I can't," she cried. "How would it look? Franco would be furious. Who would get his supper? And Beatrice—what if she found out?"

Leo hardened his gaze. "Beatrice is not living here any more. You don't have to do what she says. Just come for today, help me, and go home to Franco tonight. He won't even know."

Francesca looked towards the door. Then she looked at Leo. Her eyes softened. "I'll come, *caro*," she whispered. "I'm sorry I left it so long. Just wait a moment while I change my shoes." And she hurried out of the room.

As they walked together along the stony path, Leo's spirits began to lift. Even though he was loaded up with more sweetmeats (to tempt Marco), a goose liver, six sausages, and a bottle of bergamot and lavender, his steps were lighter and quicker than they'd been for weeks. They didn't talk much as they went. Francesca seemed lost in her own thoughts, but just the feel of her next to him, the soft swish of her skirts, gave him comfort.

He chuckled suddenly, thinking of how Marco's face would look when he saw her.

"What is it?" asked Francesca.

When Leo told her, she frowned slightly. "I hope he'll be pleased. I've always been so fond of your father. But I know he didn't want you near us after—"

Leo kicked the ground. "Only because of Beatrice."

They went on in silence, Francesca stumbling sometimes on a loose stone, Leo glad to give her his arm.

When Leo opened the door to his home and Francesca stepped inside, Marco was sitting up in bed. His mouth dropped open and he pulled up the sheets over his skinny chest. Leo saw him suck in his cheeks with shock.

"Marco, I didn't mean to give you a fright, it's all right," Francesca said all in a tumble, coming over to his bed. "How are you?"

Marco was still lying there stunned, as if someone had put a freeze spell on him. Francesca laid a hand on his cheek.

"He's still got the fever, hasn't he?" she called across to Leo. "But he's not burning up. Would you like something to eat, Marco?"

Marco managed to nod and his lips unfroze for a second into an almost-smile.

Francesca went over to the pantry where Leo was sorting the food. She looked into the pot where the soup lay in a congealed mess.

"Burned it," Leo said in a strangled voice. He could hardly speak either. It was so extraordinary to have Francesca there in the house. To see her and his father talking together like they used to. He felt little and big at the same time.

Francesca sniffed the pot. "Peacock? I think we can save it. Too good to throw away. Let's add some water and spices," and she busied herself at the cistern, ladling and pouring.

When it was ready, she put a bowl on a tray for Marco, adding a plate of goose liver and sweetmeats. While she worked, Leo thought how happy she looked, her movements sure and swift, the anxiety gone from her face.

Marco sipped the soup slowly. Sweat broke out on his forehead, and every now and then he had to stop, as if he were exhausted. But he'd drunk more than half of it before he put down his spoon.

"Now just try the goose liver," Francesca urged him. "It'll give you strength."

Afterwards, when Leo had washed Marco's dirty sheets and towels, he went to fetch more water from the well in the courtyard.

"You'll need a quantity to fill *that* bath," Francesca marveled. "You'll certainly need help just emptying the thing."

But when they came to Marco's bed, still discussing the best way to lift him, Marco let out a cry of horror.

"*Santo dio*," he trembled. "I'll not have a lady carrying me!"

"Well, I can't do it by myself, and you can wear your undergarments in the bath if you're so shy," said Leo in a determined tone.

Marco was still muttering, lying straight as a post in bed.

"Francesca's come all this way to help us, Papà. Don't be so ungrateful. She's brought herbs to put in the bath, to reduce your fever. You know that's good for you."

Marco rolled his eyes, but he sat up. "Thank you very much for coming, Francesca," he said politely. "I promise to be good."

He lifted himself slightly and tried to stand up. But his legs were so weak that he toppled back into Leo's arms. Leo grasped him under the arms and dragged him a little way across the room, with Francesca supporting his back. Then together they lifted him into the cool bath.

"Ah!" Marco was fully immersed in the water, with only his knees and head emerging. "*Splendido!*"

Leo watched him close his eyes, his shoulders relaxing against the rim of the bath.

Marco had said more in the last hour than he had for

five days. He'd actually joked! And it was all because of Francesca. Leo felt so proud and relieved he thought he might do a cartwheel right there on the floor.

After the bath, when Marco was lying on fresh sheets, Francesca brought a cup of wine mixed with water to him. She pulled a chair over and talked to him in a low voice. Leo hovered near, sweeping the floor.

"Do you forgive me?" he heard Marco whisper.

Leo swept closer.

"Of course," Francesca whispered back. "I know how hard you tried."

Marco was becoming agitated. Leo saw him twisting the sheets with his fingers.

"Rest, now, Marco," Francesca soothed. "Don't think about all that. It's done, finished. You just need to sleep, and get better."

But Marco strained towards her. Sweat beaded his upper lip.

"But do you forgive the sins of my forefathers?"

Leo stopped sweeping. *Dio!* Did Marco think he was dying? That Francesca was some kind of messenger of God, the Virgin Mary? He went over to his father and laid a hand on his cheek.

"What is it, Papà?" he urged. "Do you feel bad?"

Marco waved his hand at Leo, impatient. His eyes were still locked onto Francesca's face.

"Your father's getting himself agitated for no reason," she said. "Perhaps the bath and the talking were too much. His fever's climbing again. Leo, go and fetch my lavender oil and bring it to me, please."

Leo scurried to the bench where she'd left her things. He looked through the pantry, next to the bath. He heard whispers, voices growing louder. Where was the confounded thing?

When he returned to the bed, Marco was lying back on the sheets. He smiled as Leo dabbed his forehead with a cloth soaked in lavender. The sweat had dried and his face was peaceful. He looked profoundly relaxed.

"What did you say to him?" Leo asked Francesca.

She just put her finger to her lips and whispered, "Let him sleep now. He'll be all right."

But as Francesca got up to go, Marco grasped her hand and kissed it.

When they had gathered up her things, Leo and Francesca quietly opened the door and tiptoed outside. Dusk was deepening in the corners of the street, blurring outlines, muffling distances. Only the first star shone above them, sharp and brilliant in the tender sky.

"It's late," said Francesca. "I should be home." She gazed the length of the street. There was no one. "The law."

"I'll walk with you. We'll go quickly."

"No, no, you stay and see to Marco. I'll be less visible on my own."

"Well, I'll just walk you to the piazza. I have to see Signor Eco, anyway."

They began to hurry along the cobbled street. As they threaded their way past the quiet houses, Leo saw the moon rising over the steeple.

"You've done my father so much good," Leo began to say.

"I enjoyed being useful. He liked the sweetmeats, didn't he? Don't forget about the sausages for tomorrow."

"But just you being there, in the house with him, talking to him—it seemed to make such a difference, Francesca." Leo stopped for a moment. "What was he saying, you know, about sins, his family?"

Francesca pulled him along. "It's the fever, Leo. Sometimes he gets delirious, sees things in his mind."

They were silent as they came into the piazza. Ravens were wheeling black against the fading sky.

"Beatrice said something once," Leo rushed in. "She said I came from a family of murderers, madmen, a demon—"

"Oh, Leo, I'm sorry," Francesca turned to face him.

"Who is the demon? She said she wouldn't speak his name."

Francesca glanced away, up at the sky. The moon

hung round and dimpled above the church spire, flooding them with silver. "Full moon tomorrow night." She took a deep breath of shining air. "It is beautiful, isn't it, Leo? I haven't looked at the moon, properly, for so long."

Leo stared down at the stones. "Moonlight brings the witch," he muttered. "I hate her voice. I hate the moon."

Francesca put her face near his. "You know, when you were born, I thought your hair was made of moonlight. It shone—a little spray of silver glistened round your head. The air always seemed lighter, shinier, wherever you'd been. My sister hated it. She thinks all magic belongs to demons. But I knew then that you'd do something special in the world." She hesitated. "Perhaps you should look at the moon. Follow the voice. Maybe it will set you free. But take care, Leo, please. Be careful."

Leo stood in the middle of the piazza after she'd gone, watching the ravens fly off to roost amongst the eaves. He saw the moon rise, the dark deepen. He held Francesca's words inside him. They danced there in his mind, glittering and sparkling like coins.

But as he gazed into the moonlight, another voice came. Like fog it blew in, whispery, cold, empty. It dulled everything else, blunting hope, filling him with dread.

Whoo, Leo, it moaned, *soon...* In a corner of his mind, at the edge of his eye, he saw the mist darken into a shape. It rose up from a pit, blocking light from the sky. It stared at him with hollow eyes. There, in the depths, something flickered.

Suddenly he felt a tugging at his sleeve. The fog whirled and shifted in his head, and he heard his own name, crisp and sharp, right in his ear.

"What is it, boy? In a trance, are you?"

Leo turned to see Signor Eco looking down at him.

"Nice to see you back," grinned Signor Eco. "Thought a devil had taken your soul."

"I was just coming to see you," said Leo, "and then..."

"Well, it's past seven. I hear your father's a little better. Have you tried the juniper oil yet?"

"Yes, er, thank you—thank you very much. Did you, um, have a chance to see Merilee?"

Signor Eco smiled. "I did. Looked well and happy, too. She's made a new friend—funny little thing, looks like a boy. She said to say hello to you, and wishes your father a speedy recovery."

Leo looked down at his shoes. Was that all? Anybody could have sent that message, the butcher, the barber...

"She gave me a note for you. Said she'd put hemlock in my wine at dinner if I opened it. Look, you can check the seal—I was very obedient!"

Leo couldn't wait any more. He couldn't make small talk, ask Signor Eco how the lady with the infected toes was faring, how his trip had been. He couldn't wait until the man had gone. He tore open the red seal and devoured the words.

As his eyes reached the end of the page, it was almost more than he could bear not to race around the piazza, yelling. Joy and pure panic tore through his body like a hurricane.

Chapter Twelve

It was during the second week of her studies that Merilee began to notice the change in herself.

When Isabella told her about the properties of rose oil, coriander, or geranium—her mind opened, like the flowers themselves. She remembered names and compounds, made notes after lessons. Devil's claw soothed sore bones, myrrh eased wounds of the skin. Merilee imagined new combinations, studied particular herbs and their effects. She drew flowers of the forest in her book.

When Isabella talked to her, she listened. It was easy. She didn't stare off into space as she'd done with Beatrice. Her new teacher didn't have to call her back from that numb foggy land where nothing could touch her.

She was awake!

It was a miraculous thing, Merilee decided at the end of the second week, how a subject is colored by the person who's teaching it. When it was Aunt Beatrice talking, the most fascinating idea would turn tasteless and dull. Think! If she hadn't met Isabella, the whole world of Wisdom would have been lost to her.

Merilee hardly saw Beatrice during the week. Sometimes, after dinner, she would come to Merilee's apartment and test her on recipes for infused oils or aromatic waters. But Beatrice seemed so busy herself— holding special lectures at night, writing her own recipes—that she was always a bit distracted. She'd only stay fifteen minutes, then rush off, leaving her sentences trailing. But she did seem pleased with Merilee's improvement.

"You have got a brain in your head after all," she'd say. "I always knew it was only stubbornness. Just for a moment, you remind me of my poor dear Laura."

On the third day, when Merilee asked her how long they were going to stay at Fiesole, Beatrice suddenly became concerned about something she'd left in her apartment. "We'll talk about it tomorrow night," she called over her shoulder. And when Merilee confronted her again, she turned away to look through her notebook.

"You told my mother two weeks," Merilee went on nervously. "But I've heard that girls, well, often stay a year."

"Yes, yes, some do," Beatrice said slowly, glancing up briefly from her notebook. "And you may stay a little more than originally considered—a *fortnight*, really that's such a ridiculous portion of time, isn't it? I'll write to your mother and let her know how well I think you'll do here. But don't worry, *dear*," Beatrice gave Merilee a beaming, false smile, "I know your mother couldn't bear to be without you too long. Just imagine how pleased she'll be with her wise daughter when you go home!"

Merilee decided to be comforted by these words. It didn't seem that her aunt was planning on a whole year—and Beatrice *had* acknowledged the claims of her mother.

And if she was really honest with herself, Merilee had to admit that she was enjoying her stay. She loved the work and the company and she saw less of Beatrice than she did at home! At night, she played the recorder—often for Isabella, who would sigh wistfully throughout the sad songs. Sometimes, when entertainment was organized for the evening, Merilee was the star musician. After her performance, the audience clapped and cheered, telling her she was so talented she should play at the court of a duke!

Isabella pouted at that. "She's too good for a certain duke that *I* know."

And Beatrice was amongst the audience, smiling and nodding proudly. "Oh, yes," she'd bow modestly at all the praise, "my niece takes after me in music. I've always encouraged her. Such a pity that I never had her opportunities!"

It was only at night, just before Merilee went to sleep, that the empty feeling came. When she closed her eyes, Leo's face was there. It would begin small, the size of an acorn on a forest floor, and she'd try to look away. But the acorn always grew, until it was a tree so wide and tall that it blotted out the rest of the forest. She saw every detail of him then, as if he were there in front of her.

The empty feeling would go when she looked into his face: spirals of silver hair, golden eyes lit like suns. While she held his gaze, the landscape of her mind was full, peaceful. But then he'd call her name, and stretch out his hands towards her, and behind him, below him, a watery darkness came creeping. Soon only his head would be above the lake. The tips of his fingers. And then the dark would swallow him, seeping into all the corners of her mind as she fell through it, down into a fathomless cave.

In the morning, when she saw her desk and chair and last night's clothes flung over the arm, busy thoughts for the day began. She'd leap up and get dressed and brush her hair in the mirror. Only a twinge would come then, a splinter from the night, digging in her flesh. Leo, oh, Leo, but what can I do?

In the third week of Merilee's stay, Brigida announced that preparations should begin for the Celebration of Summer. "It will fall on the eve of the full moon, in just seven days," she said when everyone was assembled at dinner in the Green Room. She looked straight at Merilee. "The plant we have chosen to celebrate this summer is lavender. So *buon estate* to you all, and *buon lavoro!*" And she made the sign of the Order, directing her gaze at Merilee.

"It's the best night of the year," Isabella rushed in to Merilee's apartment later. "We have this enormous banquet, and lanterns are put all around the garden. There's music and dancing, and later, the iron gate is opened and we all wander into the hills with baskets, to gather up the summer flowers. It's so romantic!"

Merilee was lying on her bed, propped up on her elbow. "But why do you think she was looking at me?"

"Because this will be your night, little sweetmeat, so we'd better get started straightaway!"

Merilee sat up. "What do you mean?"

"Well, the celebration is a time for giving thanks to Mother Earth—for nourishing all her children, the plants and flowers...You know, Meri, when I'm a mother, I'm going to call my babies after my favorite flowers, that's if Alessandro agrees, of course. Imagine how lovely—Rose and Jasmine and maybe Violet—"

"And Mugwort. Isabella, what does this have to do with me in particular?"

"I'm just getting to that," Isabella sniffed. She found that Merilee often cut her off when she was right in the middle of describing something really interesting. Like yesterday, when she was talking about the new doublet Alessandro had bought for himself—scarlet, trimmed with gold lace, and he looked—

"Isabella?"

"Hmm? Oh, yes, well, this night is particularly important for you because as an Initiate, *you* will have to conduct the ceremony." Isabella giggled at Merilee's gasp of horror. "You'll have to list all the qualities of the chosen plant, and describe how it is used. That's the first stage of your training for—"

"Lavender?" Merilee was standing up now, pacing the room. "We haven't even started on lavender. I don't know the first thing about it!"

Isabella watched her pace. She smoothed a wrinkle on the bed. When Merilee came back and sat down, she said, "You'll be fine. We'll start tomorrow. You're so quick, Merilee, you remember things so well. It must run in the family."

Merilee looked at her. "Beatrice? Oh, don't say I'm like her!"

Isabella shook her head, but said nothing.

"You mean Laura? Did you ever meet her?"

Isabella nodded. "Beatrice brought her here once, just for a week. She was only young then, but everyone said how it was staggering, the way she picked it all up. She even suggested a new use for marjoram, I remember—'for when you're lonely.' I took it for a long while after she'd gone. It helped."

The two girls sat for a while in silence.

"So," Isabella finally stood up. "Let's get our beauty sleep—you'll need it much more than me, of course." She gave Merilee a cheeky grin, mincing across the floor. "And we'll start first thing in the morning. Dream of lavender, my sweet!"

But as Merilee climbed into bed, she remembered Leo's voice at twilight, down by the lake. "Lavender," he'd said. "Say you're late because you were collecting *lavender*."

So she dreamt of Leo that night; Leo and the lake, the dark coming down, and the smell of lavender everywhere.

As the days passed, Merilee felt more confident about the Celebration of Summer. She was almost looking forward to it. Isabella made the evening sound so special, and the rustle of excitement amongst the women— cooking delicious things, making decorations —was contagious. Every time she walked past the kitchen, some wonderful smell made her nostrils quiver, but she was never allowed in.

"It's a surprise," the women would say, barring the door with their aproned bellies.

The servants were sworn to secrecy too. "We don't even have a hint of the menu," Consuela complained to

Merilee. "They won't let us help!" Consuela didn't seem to know whether to be outraged or delighted at having her kitchen kidnapped.

And the studies were going well. Lavender was such a wonderful plant. Soothing, healing—Merilee felt almost affectionate towards it, as if it were a good, reliable friend.

It was strange, she thought, that as her knowledge deepened, she remembered more about Laura, too; what she was like when they were younger, conversations they'd had. She remembered how Laura liked to talk about the forest, her eyes shining when she came back with wild parsley or jasmine. She'd collect the flowers and leaves of plants and press them in her book. When they were dried, she'd sketch them, showing all their parts in brilliant detail. She even listened to Beatrice without fidgeting.

"How can you *stay* with Aunt Beatrice?" she remembered asking Laura when she was only four or five.

"I like the plants," Laura had replied. "And Aunty's a bit nicer to me, Meri. I know it's not fair, but when you're older, you'll find her easier to get along with too."

Once, when Merilee had got into trouble about something, Laura had cuddled her and said, "Aunty's just an old bumblebee—buzz buzz. But Mamma and Papà love us to the stars and back, and they're the most important, aren't they?" Merilee had gone to sleep in her sister's bed, warm and safe.

At Fiesole, in just the last few weeks, Merilee felt as if she'd found something of her sister again. But the memories sharpened her loss. "Add six drops of marjoram to your soup," she imagined Laura saying to her. "For when you're lonely."

On the Wednesday morning before the Celebration, she was going down to breakfast when Isabella met her in the hall. "Come with me," she whispered. "*Ssh!*" She tugged Merilee back into her apartment and closed the door.

"What is it? You know how Beatrice hates us to be late."

"Look," said Isabella. She pulled off her headband and the false hair fell down her back.

"I've seen it before, Isabella," sighed Merilee. "It's growing back, isn't it?"

"No, silly!" Isabella was picking at her headband. From under the threading she pulled a piece of paper. "This is for you, sweetness. A man has come, someone you know—Signor Eco. He has a message for you."

"For me?"

"From *Leo!*" Isabella's voice was hushed. "The signor gave me the note because we were talking—he's ancient, of course, but he has very elegant manners—anyway, he decided to take me into his confidence, seeing as you and I are such friends."

Merilee fingered the seal. She didn't hear a word

Isabella was saying. Her heart was loud in her ears.

"Here." Isabella offered her a knife to cut the seal. "This is the most romantic thing that's ever happened," she sighed. "What does he say? Is he pining to death without you?"

Merilee read the letter. She looked up at Isabella.

"Oh, Meri, what is it?" Isabella snatched up the letter and her eyes raced over it. "The poor boy," she said.

Merilee read the letter again. She touched the "W" that was smudged. She closed her eyes, imagining him all alone in his house, worrying for his father.

"I must go to him," she said to Isabella.

At breakfast, Merilee saw Signor Eco walk in with Beatrice. She had her arm through his, her mouth near his ear, talking without pause as they walked towards a table. Quickly, Merilee steered Isabella in the same direction until they were almost running through the Yellow Room.

"Ah, young Merilee," cried Signor Eco as he pulled out a chair next to him. "Sit here with me. It's nice to see a friendly face from home. *Another* friendly face, I should say," he added hastily as Beatrice frowned at him.

"I was just telling Signor Eco how well my niece is doing, here at Fiesole," Beatrice said loudly.

Brigida, who was sitting opposite, gave one of her vague smiles.

Beatrice turned to the apothecary. "You must stay for our Celebration of Summer, Alberto," Beatrice cried, clapping her hands. "It's a splendid night, and my Merilee will conduct the ceremony."

Brigida looked up, her brows raised.

"That is, of course, if our Head is agreeable," Beatrice hurried on, growing flustered, "and actually, come to think of it, perhaps—"

"The Celebration of Summer is a ritual of the Wise Women of Fiesole," Brigida said quietly. "As welcome as Signor Eco is to share our table and buy our wares, the other is a more private matter. I'm surprised you've forgotten that, Beatrice," and she made a swift sign of the Order.

Beatrice signed back, her face red. "Yes indeed, I'm quite carried away with the excitement of it all, do forgive me, what with my niece being the *Initiate* this year." She puffed out her chest and said to Signor Eco in a loud whisper, "That's the first stage to being my assistant, you know."

Merilee looked at her aunt. She heard the steely confidence under her whisper, saw the determined tilt of her chin. Beatrice wasn't going to allow anything to get in her way—not Merilee's wishes, nor Francesca's pleas. When she was Head, she'd probably change all the rules anyway. Merilee could see her itching to start. She'd ask the whole world to the ceremonies, just to show off her power.

Beware of Beatrice, Merilee, Leo had written. *She speaks with a forked tongue.*

How could she have believed that Beatrice would ever let her go?

"Ask him *now*," Isabella hissed into her ear.

Merilee glanced at Signor Eco. He was fiddling with his egg, making patterns with the yolk. He looked uncomfortable, as if he would love to be anywhere but at a table where he was being uninvited to a celebration.

Beatrice was tucking into her breakfast with enthusiasm.

Merilee gently tugged at Signor Eco's gown. As he turned to her, she whispered, "I want to write a note to Leo. Will you come to Workshop 4 in an hour?"

Signor Eco nodded and returned his gaze to his plate, where the egg had congealed into a sticky yellow crust.

"Mmm," said Beatrice heartily, wiping her mouth, "nothing like a robust meal to start the day!"

Back in her apartment, Merilee took a new quill and began her letter. She was shaking with anxiety. Now that she'd decided to do this, it seemed too big, impossible for her to do alone. It would be the most daring thing she'd ever considered.

She sat back in her chair, the quill suspended between her fingers.

"If you wait for Burrweed to send you home, you'll

be so rickety and old you'll have forgotten where he lives," Isabella said. Her tone was dry, but her voice wobbled.

Merilee looked at her. Isabella wiped her eyes with the back of her hand.

"You've got to do it, Meri. It's just that I'll miss you so." She gave a loud sniff. "Remember, the gate will be opened for the Celebration of Summer."

Needles of alarm raced along Merilee's skin. "Yes," she said quietly. "That's when I'll go."

Isabella nodded. "It's your best chance."

Dear You, wrote Merilee, taking a deep breath, *I hope by the time this reaches you that your father is much better. But I will see you soon, because I'm going to ESCAPE!*

Isabella breathed over her shoulder. "Tell him neither wolves nor bandits nor ghosts of the night will keep you from him."

"Oh, Isabella."

But now Merilee pictured herself creeping into the dark of the forest, alone, and shuddered. Maybe she'd take her knife with her.

Meet me at our tree on Saturday afternoon. We'll tell each other everything then.

M.

P.S. Give your father lavender oil, massaged into his skin three times a day.

"Hmm," said Isabella as Merilee folded the letter and

sealed it, "a short, *sensible* letter. I, of course, would have written it differently."

"Of course," Merilee gave her friend a watery grin, and the two girls walked down the stairs with their arms tightly linked, as if they never wanted to let each other go.

On the evening of the Celebration, the garden was drenched in moonlight as the women sat down to eat. It bleached the creamy linen tablecloths white, puddled in the silver bowls. The air was warm, so still that the candles at each table barely flickered. Merilee gazed around at the beauty of it. The loud bursts of chatter, the jugs of wine, the warm glances of the women. She wanted to remember all of it, forever.

She slipped off her clogs and felt the grass crush underfoot. Eve of the full moon, she told herself, marveling, and don't I *feel* like Eve tonight, stepping out into this garden of paradise?

Whenever the thought came of what she had to do later, a little stab of fear dug in, right under her rib cage. But for now, she was hungry.

After two hours of speaking—she had performed the ritual welcome for summer (and all in the right order, thank heaven!) and made her speech about lavender (Brigida had actually said *"Bravissima!"* and showed her a real smile)—the smell of the young deer roasting on the spit made her stomach growl. On the table there were bowls of steaming rabbit and lamb baked with mushrooms, and small mountains of nuts and fruit.

Merilee grinned at Isabella as she came up with a dish of meat from the spit.

"You were wonderful tonight," said Isabella, forking two slices onto Merilee's plate. But the skin of her face was tight and drawn.

"We'll find a way to see each other again," Merilee said softly.

Isabella sat down next to her. "I'm losing two people tonight."

"What do you mean?"

"I just heard that the duke is sending Alessandro away. Tomorrow—at dawn. Maria told me she heard one of his servants ordering the carriage."

"Oh, Isabella!" Merilee put an arm around her shoulders. "That's terrible. Where is he going?"

"Padua. How many days' ride is that from here? The duke says Alessandro has to stop frittering his time away—with me, of course—and start studying at the university." Isabella put her head in her hands.

"Well, Alessandro just shouldn't go. He should stand up to his father!"

"How?" Isabella said wearily. The energy was gone from her face. "The duke would cut him off, stop his allowance. What will he live on?" She smiled bleakly for a moment. "Love is enough for me. But not for a duke's son, I'm afraid."

Later, when the women went inside to collect their baskets, Merilee hurried to her apartment and took out her best red velvet dress. She folded it into the bottom of her basket, together with the silk girdle. Hesitating for a moment, she undid the catch of the gold necklace her mother had given her when she was born. Her sister's had been just the same, with the single pearl like a teardrop. She hid the necklace in the folds of the red dress. Then she placed her recorder in with the clothes and laid a blanket over the whole. The other dresses she would leave for Isabella...

As the women filed out through the great gate, into the forest, Merilee looked back. She saw the Academy where she'd lived for nearly four weeks. There was the window of her room, and further along, Isabella's. It was suddenly very dear to her, this place, where so many things had happened for the first time.

"Come along, don't linger," Merilee felt a poke in her back. "You should be first in line."

Beatrice urged her along. She gave a lantern to Merilee. "You did very well tonight, Merilee. Now see if you can be the one to gather the most lavender—and fill that basket of yours!"

Beatrice gave her a hearty smile. She was trying to be

nice, Merilee realized with a shock. There was a sort of plea in her tone. Laura must have seen that smile sometimes. Had she seen how desperate their aunt was, too? How much Beatrice depended on them? Maybe Laura had always known that.

A wave of sadness passed over Merilee then, but whether it was for Laura, or her lonely aunt, or the good-bye she would have to say to her friend, she didn't know.

Merilee was soon far out in front, gathering distance from the group as she hurried down the hill. The women behind her were stopping every now and then to chat, their lanterns making small pockets of brightness in the black.

Ahead lay the silence of the forest. Merilee wanted to be back in that soft tinkle of women's talk, dawdling amongst the lavender. For a moment, she could hardly breathe with the longing.

"Psst!"

Merilee peered into the darkness.

"I just wanted to say goodbye, sweetmeats. It's so hard to let you go!"

Isabella ran out of a pool of shadows and hugged her. They clung together for a moment, until Isabella wrenched herself free. "Be careful, Meri. Walk fast until you're out of the forest, no matter how tired you are. Here, I brought you the carving knife from tonight. Keep it in your basket."

Merilee fingered it gingerly. "Thanks, Isabella. *Ti voglio bene.*"

"Me too," whispered Isabella. "Good luck!" And she was gone, darting back into the trees.

Merilee stumbled forward, tears coursing down her face. She clutched her lantern, the basket bumping rhythmically at her hip. Soon she could hear no murmur of voices, nor see any flicker of lights. She was alone in the forest, with just the moonlight making shadows on the ground.

Merilee walked on through clusters of cypress trees, pines and olive groves. She tried to name the plants and vegetation she saw, testing herself on how much she'd learned. It was best not to look further than the bushes and trees just ahead of her.

When she came to a vineyard, she stopped for just a minute. The moon was high in the sky now, and grapes glistened on the vine. She picked a small bunch. It was comforting to see each vine tied so carefully to its stick. Someone had done that right here—watered it and watched it grow. She thought about that as she ate the grapes.

Trees closed in again as she left the vineyard. Only scarce drops of moonlight trickled between the branches. Merilee sang under her breath—silly songs Isabella and she had made up late at night. But her legs ached and she was so tired behind her eyes that her lids stung in the night air.

When she came to a little stone altar, built on the side of the hill, she decided to sit down and rest for a while. The candle in her lamp had almost burned down, but in the flickering glow she saw the small statue of a Madonna inside the altar. The hands were clasped in prayer, the smile contented. I'll lie near her for a while, thought Merilee, and looked around for a smooth patch of ground. A soft mound of grass lay just behind the altar, making a good pillow. Just for a few minutes, she told herself, and closed her eyes.

She must have fallen asleep only for a second, because she had a swift sensation of dropping from a cliff—and then she woke, her heart hammering. Someone was crouched at the altar. A man in a dark cloak was reaching in towards the statue. Peering around, she saw another man, bigger, bulkier, coming up behind him.

"Have you got it?" asked the bigger man, watching.

Merilee held her breath, the blood roaring in her ears.

The first man was pulling something out from behind the Madonna. It must have caught because he swore softly. Then the thing was free and glittering in the moonlight.

"Good place to hide it, eh, Carlo? That'll fetch a fortune!"

Merilee turned around in silence on her knees. She started to crawl away, up the hill, but her knee struck a sharp stone or twig and a gasp of pain broke from her throat. In a second, the men were there, leaping on her, grappling her to the ground.

The cloaked man held her down by the shoulders. He thrust his face over hers. She could smell the garlic and meat on his breath. "And what have *you* got for us then, girlie?"

His hands were on her throat. Big hard hands. She could feel the callouses on his palms. His fingers met and overlapped round her neck.

"Snap you like a stick, couldn't I?"

Merilee's fingers scrabbled along the dirt. She felt the handle of her basket. Now the rough wool of the blanket. Under, under, deeper, below the dress, in there, the sharp point of the knife.

"Look here!" shouted the bigger man, and he leaned over and flicked Merilee's hand from the basket. He pulled out the gold necklace from underneath the red velvet dress, and dangled it on the edge of the knife.

"Well, little lady, how kind of you to bring us your jewelry. We've collected quite a treasure tonight, eh, Carlo?"

Merilee felt the man's hands loosen around her throat as he turned to examine the necklace. She tried to sit up, but the man Carlo pushed her down, hard.

Her mind was blank with terror. She stared at the dark. And then one of Isabella's songs stole into her mind. It was a witchy song, nightmarish—they'd made it up to scare each other. She began to chant it, a whisper at first, and then louder, as loud as the blood screaming in her veins.

> *Hemlock, mandrake, seed of fire,*
> *Bring Black Death, a funeral pyre.*
> *Mugwort, nightshade, the devil's eye,*
> *Drink my brew, scum, choke and die!*

Carlo was backing away on his knees, staring at her, a hand still gripping her ankle. She sat upright, pushing towards him until her eyes were level with his. Joining her index fingers together, she made the sign of the Order, pointing straight and spearlike at his forehead.

"*Hemlock, mandrake, seed of fire,*" she chanted.

"Carlo," hissed the second man. He pointed to the basket. On the leather clasp there was the wing-shaped W of the Order.

Merilee heard Carlo draw in his breath. The other man then held up the knife, the gold necklace still hanging from it. He showed the handle where the sign was engraved in silver.

"Wise Women, Carlo, she's one of them—she's putting a spell on us."

"*Bring Black Death, a funeral pyre...*" Merilee murmured on, as if in a trance.

"They're witches, I've heard it, they drink bat's blood—"

"They can kill a pig just by looking at it—"
"Steal your manhood—"

> *Wise Women, witches, devil's work we do,*
> *Mixing up the poisons of a demon's brew—*

Merilee felt the blood pounding through her heart as she chanted. But she held her voice strong and low, and as she sang the rushing fear began to flower into a fire of exhilaration that spread through her veins like wine.

She watched the men crawl away, their hands raised in terror. The necklace dropped in the grass, the knife was thrown point down in the dirt. Still she kept chanting, making the sign at them as they retreated down the hill.

Then she gathered up her necklace and knife and the red velvet dress, packing them all into the basket. She was so awake now, she could have marched to Florence and back one hundred and fifty times.

Chapter Thirteen

"How do you feel this morning?" Leo asked his father as soon as he woke up.

"What day is it?"

"Saturday."

"Has a whole week gone by?"

"Almost. Would you like a cup of water?"

"Yes, please. Was Francesca here, or did I dream it?"

Leo called back from the cistern in the kitchen. "Yesterday. She came and brought you some food. You talked with her."

Marco nodded, satisfied. "I thought so. It was a lovely dream. The best I've had for years."

Leo watched him drink. "It was real, Papà, and she seemed to make you happy."

Marco nodded. "I've had some terrible dreams, Leo. That voice, always moaning on, creeping in like rain under the door. Did you hear it, son?" He leaned forward and grasped Leo's wrist. "You mustn't listen to it, do you hear me? Even if it calls your name."

Marco let go of Leo and slumped back against the pillows. He was panting, the breath coming hard and shallow from his chest.

"You've talked too much, Papà," Leo said, smoothing his sheets. "It's exhausted you."

"But I am better, aren't I, Leo?"

Leo leaned over him and felt his cheek. It was warm, but dry. "I'm sure you are. And now I'm going to give you a nice massage with lavender oil."

Marco closed his eyes. "Thank you, son." But he was asleep again by the time Leo came back with the oil.

Leo knew that his father had slept well last night, because Leo had been awake all night himself. At least that's what it had felt like. How could he sleep, when there was so much to think about? He pictured Merilee wandering in the dark by herself. And he tossed about in the tangled sheets, the moonlight flooding in, waiting— for what?

Leo, the voice moaned, at the very edge of his mind, almost there, at his toes, like the tide coming in. Like the eve of a full moon.

Leo took out Merilee's letter again. He'd slept with it in his hand, and the ink was a little smeared. Only a few hours until he would see her. It was hard to believe.

First, he'd go to market. Then he'd prepare the day's meals and make sure his father had something to eat. He really did seem better today—a bit confused, maybe, but alert. I'll tell Papà I'm going to the apothecary's shop, he decided, to get some more supplies.

A bolt of alarm shot up his spine. He leaped up and began dressing for market. He didn't want to think about how long he'd be away. Or what on earth he and Merilee were going to *do*—today, and for the rest of their lives! Where do you go when you've escaped and you can't go home?

Leo found Merilee sound asleep on a bed of pine needles. Her dark hair was spread out on something soft and red. He crept up and crouched by her side. He looked into her face. Tears stung behind his eyes. Her mouth was slightly open, her arm flung out. She looked so trusting, so vulnerable, like a very young child at home asleep in her room.

Quietly, Leo put his basket down near hers. He'd brought oranges and a bag of figs, a slab of cheese, and a flask of wine. She'll be starving, he'd thought, after a night and day in the forest.

"Leo!"

He swung around and there she was, awake, jumping up, arms circling his waist and her cheek pressed hard against his.

"I'm so glad to see you, Leo."

"Merilee! Let me look at you. You were so brave—how did you get over the wall?"

"I went through the gate, easy as you please. How's your father? Did you give him the lavender rub?"

"Yes—he seems a bit stronger today. But he hasn't been out of bed for six days. It's been terrible."

"Oh, Leo, I wish I'd been there to help. But I've learned so much, maybe I'd be more use now..."

Leo spread out a rug on the ground and tugged at Merilee's hand. "Come and eat and tell me everything. What's it been like with old batface? Did she lock you up at night?"

Merilee grinned. "Well no, not exactly," and she took a fig and then another and began trying to describe for Leo the different, strange world of Fiesole.

As he listened, Leo watched Merilee's face. It was full of light and expression, you could see she was living the moments she was telling, and she laughed more easily, throwing back her head as she talked about the girl, Isabella, and the splendid musical evenings they'd had.

"You would have been so proud of me," she told him, "I was the star musician!"

When Leo asked for a tune, she hunted through her basket. As she pulled out the recorder, the knife came with it.

"Did you have to use this?" Leo picked it up and felt the sharp edge with his finger.

"All in a night's work, my friend!" Merilee grabbed the knife from him and brandished it in the air like a pirate.

Leo gazed at Merilee in admiration. She used the knife to cut off chunks of cheese, washing it down with a cup of cold wine. Leo diced up an orange and they talked until they were hoarse. Then they lay back on the rug, feeling the warm breeze drift over them.

Merilee's eyes were closing. She looked so relaxed. But they had no time. They needed to make plans. Weren't the shadows under the trees already a little longer?

"Have you thought what you're going to do now?" Leo asked softly.

"Well," Merilee drawled sleepily, "I *was* going to help you with your father—"

"But after, in the future—I mean, you can't go back to Fiesole now."

"No." Merilee sat up.

"You could come home with me. Papà would understand. I'd make him understand."

Merilee shook her head. "You couldn't hide me there forever. Beatrice would shout the house down." She straightened her back. "Leo, if your father was still dangerously ill, I'd risk it, and raspberries to old batface."

Merilee grinned suddenly. "That's why I broke out of prison, after all. But he's recovering now, isn't he—and you know, I did a lot of thinking while I was walking last night." Merilee took a breath, but didn't say any more.

Leo picked up a twig and broke it. "Are you going to your mother then? She's missed you so much."

Merilee began putting things back in her basket. "Beatrice will be there, I'm sure of it. I'll see Mamma later, when it's the right time." She stood up and brushed the crumbs from her skirt. She turned to face Leo. She wasn't sleepy any more.

"Let's run away to Venice, Leo," she said, "like we always dreamt."

Leo stared at her.

"I could play the recorder, be a traveling musician. I'm sure I'd be good enough—they said I could play at court!—and for extra money I could always help in an apothecary shop."

"But Merilee—" Leo didn't know where to start. "I couldn't leave my father, not now. He seems better, but he's so fragile still. I couldn't leave him on his own."

Merilee nodded. "Of course, not until he's strong. But you could meet me there—it may only be a few weeks before you're ready."

Leo's heart raced. He felt torn, broken down the middle like the twig he'd just snapped. He thought of his father crying out in the night. He saw Merilee running off into a new life, her hair streaming behind her. And he heard the voice calling him, pulling at the edges of him, *Leo, help, Leo...*

Merilee put her hand on his arm. "Don't you want to break free, Leo? Remember how often you've said that to me? All the rules, the laws, the scary stories. All our life they've told us what to do, forbidden us to see each other. Well, now I'm going to do what *I* want to do."

She wound up her dark hair and fixed it on top of her head. As she stretched up, the whole length of her rippled in Leo's mind. How changed she was, he thought, so clear and certain, like a knife edge. Leo remembered how she'd looked when he'd first found her asleep. He half wished...

"You know, at Fiesole, for just a moment," Merilee's eyes were fixed on his face, "I got a glimpse of what my life could be like. I was playing at a concert in the Green Room, and it was as if these great heavy shutters behind my eyes opened just a crack, and a brilliant light shone in. It was only for a second, but I still remember that feeling. I was really alive, I was so bathed in light I could have floated into the air. That was *me*, I thought. That's who I am!"

Leo nodded. He'd had that feeling when he was practicing his magic—when he first saw deep inside something. But it was so long since he'd done that. These days, he felt like a dull piece of wood.

He glanced away, down at the shadows on the ground. He could hear Merilee breathing beside him, feel her waiting for him. His heart constricted. He was failing her, he thought. He imagined the mouse that must live in his heart, scampering around in terror.

Then, in the silence between them there came the sound of bushes rustling. Something was moving.

Leo and Merilee froze.

Leo grabbed the two baskets and Merilee's hand and began to run down the hill. They went crashing through the trees, hurtling over rocks, until they came to a clump of shrubs woven tightly together in a low wall. They flung themselves down behind it. Their breath was loud in the silence.

"Let's go down to the lake," whispered Merilee. "I'm not afraid of the witch any more. No one will follow us there."

"But it's full moon tonight," Leo whispered back. "Maybe you should be afraid."

Merilee looked at him. "The witch will get you, look out, look out, Snakes in her hair..."

Leo gazed back at her. Between them, they held all their childhood. But it was only Leo Pericolo who heard the voice now, gathering strength with the dusk. It seemed as if the witch were singling him out, sending her challenge to him alone.

"All right," he said wearily, "let's go."

They went quietly and quickly. When Merilee stopped to listen, she heard nothing.

"It may have been just a pheasant or a peacock," she said. But they hurried on until the trees began to thin and they reached the pebbly shore.

A gusty wind had sprung up, rippling the surface of the lake.

"Can't you hear the voice now, Merilee?" asked Leo.

But Merilee was flinging off her shoes. The wind tore the words from her mouth. The water trickled over her toes. Behind them, the sun was sinking, the sky flaming.

Leo put his hands over his ears. But it didn't stop the voice. *Whoo pheye, Leo,* Leo!

He watched Merilee playing with the water, daring it, and her mouth was moving as if she was saying something. But he couldn't hear anything, not a word of it. He held his head and it hurt, the voice scraping at the back of his teeth, inside his mouth, behind his eyes. It was white in his head, cloudy like smoke, and there, etched in black, came that face with the hollow eyes.

Merilee was mouthing something at him, laughing—"hide and seek!"—was *that* what she was saying? And she was running away, beckoning for him to follow, racing towards the rocks at the southern edge. He watched her go, hair flying in the wind, and he'd never felt so far away from her. She couldn't hear the voice like he did. She was playing, laughing! The moan was only for him now, seeking him out, punishing him. She could only hear the wind ripping at the trees.

He began to run after her. He couldn't bear to be alone with the voice. But as he ran, the moaning moved with him, there, just under his heartbeat.

When he reached the rocky cliffs, Merilee had disappeared.

He scrambled over the rocks, calling her name. Then he tripped on a sharp stone and fell heavily, skinning his knee. He crouched there for a while, sucking the blood from his graze, watching the great cliffs throw their shadows over the water.

He looked out across the lake. The water was melting into the sky. Dusk was already blurring outlines, graying edges. The rocky promontory that jutted out at the end of the southern cliffs was hardly visible. It could have been a freakish wave rolling back towards the cliff.

"Merilee, Meri*lee!*" Leo began to run blindly, stabbing his feet on the stones. Oh, where was she? And then, far off, he heard a piercing voice, Merilee's, and he picked his way over the rocks towards it, hanging onto the sound as if it were a rope that would save him from drowning.

She was standing under an overhanging rock, deep in the shadows. But as he drew near, he saw her emerge, her face lit by a flickering light, and behind her there was a tunnel of utter darkness.

She showed him the oil lamp she'd found. "It was in here—oh, Leo, come and look, it's a cave, all made up like a sitting room! Someone must have lived here once."

Leading him inside, she put the lamp down on the ground. "See," Merilee sounded excited, "this old tinderbox was dry. It was left carefully on the ledge here. And look, these are silk cushions, rotting a bit with the damp floor, but you can still sit on them."

Leo took the lamp. The voice had quietened. It seemed muffled by the air in the cave, which was thicker, warm and salty. Leo sniffed. He could smell candle grease and incense. On the ledge there were two cups and a jar beside a neatly folded stack of blankets.

It was all just as he'd imagined. Everything was as his father had described. He held the lamp up to the rock wall above. He looked at it very hard for a long time. And the wall began to move.

The minerals in the limestone were separating, sparkling singly like far-flung stars. He could see the form and shape of each, and the rock face behind became a swirling galaxy of light. Leo put the lamp down. He didn't need it any more. In the stone, he saw the flames of ancient fires, and figures dancing through them. He could see back in time, back to when the first creatures were evolving. The stone showed him horned animals and tiny hopping insects, men hunting, sleeping. The light was so bright that he scrunched up his eyes for a moment, but a golden glow still seeped through his lids.

"Leo, bring the lamp over here." Merilee was peering at the wall opposite.

Leo was listening to the quiet. In the glowing spaces that filled his mind, the moan had become just a whisper.

"Quickly, Leo, come *on!* There's something drawn on the rock."

On the eastern wall, the lamp showed a painting of a woman's face. It was a very worn fresco, eaten away by time and moisture, and yet the face looked so familiar...

"Francesca!" cried Leo. But even as he spoke, he saw the strong line of the chin, the black mark on the cheek.

"No, her grandmother, Caterina," Merilee said quietly. She brought the lamp down to the words written at the bottom.

"For my beautiful Caterina," they read together. "Eternal love, *amore per sempre*, Illuminato." But the last words were crossed through with a heavy line, and next to them, in huge thick letters, was "Die, you witch!"

Leo took the lamp from Merilee. He was trembling, making the lamp jiggle. He stared at the words leaping out at him from the wall. Words his father had never wanted him to see.

"The sins of my forefathers," he whispered.

"Leo, what is it?"

"Nothing." Leo brushed a hand across his eyes.

Merilee took the lamp from him and put it on the

ledge. "Something to do with light," she murmured to herself. Then she turned suddenly and faced Leo. "Your great-grandfather, Manton's father, what was his name?"

"Illuminato," murmured Leo, still staring at the words.

"Well, he must have been in love with my great-grandmother. Oh, Leo, it's quite romantic really."

Leo turned away in disgust. "What kind of love was that, to write those words underneath?" He kicked away the cushion at his feet.

Merilee glanced back at the wall. "I don't think he wrote that bit, Leo. See, the letters are all heavy and thick, and they're leaning backwards. It's quite a different style altogether."

She doesn't *want* to think he wrote that bit, thought Leo. Neither do I, Leo whispered to himself. *Neither do I.* But dread was hardening like ice in his stomach.

Merilee was still puzzling. "He must have been a very passionate man. I wonder why they didn't marry. I know my great-grandmother died when her children were still quite young. At least, everyone presumed she was dead, because she disappeared. There was an outbreak of plague in the village, Mamma told us, and lots of people fled. But why," Merilee said more slowly, "didn't she take the children?"

She stopped suddenly and Leo glanced at her. He saw her eyes widen as she stared at the ground. His eyes followed hers. There, at his feet, in the clean pale space where the cushion had been, lay a gold necklace. It was broken at the clasp, but a single pearl was still attached to it.

Sweat broke out on Leo's forehead. The voice was returning, thudding in his ears.

"Laura's necklace!" said Merilee.

She bent to pick it up. It lay cradled in her hand. Merilee's fingers curled over it, making a fist. "My sister has been here, Leo." She stared at him, searching his face.

Leo turned and began to hobble towards the entry. The pain in his head was too much. Suddenly Merilee pulled him back, her hand over his mouth.

"Someone's outside," she hissed in his ear. "Don't make a sound."

She dragged him against the wall, into the shadows. "What if it's Beatrice? Oh, *dio*, where shall we go? We're trapped!" Her lips were white and trembling, all the playfulness gone.

Leo swung round and faced the dark opening at the back of the cave.

"Oh, Leo, not in there, we don't know where it leads."

He picked up the lamp. "I think I have to find out."

Merilee put her hand into his.

But Leo slid away. "I don't know if I can keep you safe, Merilee."

"Just *run*," she cried, as a gull screamed from the rocks outside, and Leo, holding up the lamp, lunged into the darkness with Merilee right behind him.

They raced through the narrow tunnel, the lamp sputtering, making just a small glow in front of their feet. The dark was so thick, and the air so musty, that it was like being sealed into a grave.

"We must be nearly right through," panted Leo, not slowing down. His lungs hurt. No crack of light showed behind them or in front.

"What if there's no way out?" breathed Merilee. "We can't go back."

They scurried along the winding path so black that Merilee couldn't see her hand in front of her. Blindly she sped after Leo, holding tightly to his tunic. He pulled her through gaps where they both had to turn sideways and feel their way along.

Leo heard a squeaking and a scurrying as a rat ran over their feet.

Merilee screamed, but Leo called back to her. "That's a water rat—I think we may be near the exit."

As they turned a corner, so sharp and narrow that Leo nearly ran face first into the wall, he saw a twinkle of light far off ahead of them.

"There!" he cried and they ran faster, feeling cooler air on their faces, hearing the wind gusting now through the widening space.

They burst out of the cave like stones hurtling from a sling. But they stopped dead. Surrounded by water, they were standing at the edge of a slim finger of land that reached right out into the middle of the lake.

"The promontory," whispered Leo. "We've run the whole stretch of it underground." Less than a step from their feet, the rocky surface dropped straight into the lake.

Chapter Fourteen

"Step back, Merilee." Leo loosened her hold on his hand. "Get away from the edge—quick!"

The full moon shivered over the water. It threw down nets of silver, catching little waves cresting in the wind.

Leo was waiting. He listened to the voice roaring up at him from the lake. He heard it riding the moonlight, whining on the wind. Inside, he was completely still, silent in the eye of his hurricane.

Merilee scrambled over the rocks. She crouched a small distance away, her eyes fixed on Leo. The water tossed around him. Far away on the pebbly shore, she saw waves frothing white in the moonlight.

"Stay where you are!" Leo called to Merilee. "Don't move."

His eyes didn't stray from the water. He knew it would be soon. Just a heartbeat away. The moon beamed down on the greasy surface of the lake, bright as day. But the light was cold and steely with no warmth in it, only menace.

And now he saw where the water was swirling, spiraling like oil sucked into a vortex. There, right near his feet, down where the ripples were growing bigger, the lake was opening. Moonlight swept across a pit of blackness, a nothingness so terrible it sucked the air from his lungs.

And a howling filled the air, as if the voice of the wind and the moonlight and the dark emptiness below all condensed into this one sound. Leo screamed as the voice ripped open the silence inside him. He heard his cry mingle with the sound and his legs trembled against the swirling pull of the pit. The emptiness sucked at his toes, wrenched at his hair, his eyes. He crouched down, clinging onto the rock until the skin bled against the sharp little shells and his knuckles whitened.

Then the water fell back as the witch rose up, out of the dark.

At first, she was only a shadow against the night. Huge as a giant, tall as the mast of a ship, she towered above him. No moonlight picked at the surface of her. She was darkness knitted together, a thousand nights sewed into a blackness without stars.

Leo felt the air clot around his face as he was drawn near. The darkness of her was blinding, irresistible. Leo's eyes stung and watered. His nails tore against the rock.

"Don't listen to her!" he remembered his father crying. But the witch called to him. Her darkness would cover him. It offered everything and nothing, no light nor shade, no pain. As he looked, he knew what it would be like to die, or never be born.

His hands let go of the rock. He stood up. He reached out, as if his arms were not his own. His fingertips met something colder than ice. All feeling began to seep away, so that his torn nails, the bleeding skin of his hands, no longer existed for him. The numbness spread up into his shoulders, his neck. He could no longer turn his head or look away. And then he saw that the dark of her was brightening where he'd touched her, and the moonlight played over her valleys and hills, picking her out from the night.

And as he looked, an enormous grief rose up in him. It was a wave in his belly like hunger, hunger for something he could never have nor change. Her face in the moonlight was beautiful—so dear and familiar, like the face of Francesca, his mother of comfort, and as she smiled at him the light shivered as it did over the water, making the smile different. There was something behind it now, a teasing, an anger, and he was looking instead at the woman painted on the wall of the cave. Caterina.

A terrible wailing filled his ears. The sound twisted the guts in his belly till he didn't know if the cry came from inside him or out. Leo watched, just as Illuminato must have done so long ago when he caused the lovely face in front of him to transform.

Leo reached out to stop it—he tried to see behind the dark.

Illuminato!

The cry seemed to come from the bottom of the lake. It boomed all around him, rippling the water, deafening him. The head of her reared up, a tongue lashing out of the mouth. It forked like lightning, lapping at his lips, his chin, his eyes. Her tongue was a piece of darkness and wherever she licked his skin, the pain drifted away.

Numbness stole into his heart and he no longer cared that he'd lost the power of his vision, that the twin signs he'd been born with were no match for the magic of his ancestor.

"Yes," he whispered as the dark drifted in. He could just fall, melt into a universe that existed before time.

"Leo, come back!"

Merilee's voice slapped at the back of his neck.

Leo flinched awake.

He was looking into the hollows of the witch's eyes. Something flickered against the dark. And he knew, then, that he had to go in there.

He wouldn't go blindly. He'd move in while he held himself still. He'd watch the witch's dreams while he stayed awake.

But he longed to fall blind, into her darkness.

"Leo!"

Merilee's breath was warm in his ear. She was pulling at his belt.

"Go back!" he cried, swinging round and pushing her away. "I can't protect you here!" He watched her pick herself up and scurry up to the rocks. As he turned back to the lake, a tendril of fog floated into his mind, dulling the small glow of his power.

Leo ground his teeth. He couldn't afford to think about Merilee. He stared hard into the pits of the witch's eyes, and tried to remember himself as he was in the forest. He remembered how he'd seen into the heart of things, easy as breathing. How time had dissolved, like wine in water. He remembered the cave, and the dance of the animals. And slowly, the golden truth of the cave filtered into his mind, and he held the glow still, guiding it just as he'd done with the lamp, while he gazed into the tunnels behind the witch's eyes.

Shadows and ducking shapes flitted past him as he searched. He drifted deeper and deeper into the dark, his heart trembling with the fear of losing his way. But still he went forward, wading through terror that clung like quicksand. As he moved into the heart of the tunnel, the glow of his power grew and in the golden light of it he saw a child's face.

Green-eyed, red-haired, just for a second he

glimpsed it, and then another came and another, flying through corridors of darkness, such little sobbing creatures that the witch had taken. Wisps of their garments caught in his light—sky blue, scarlet—they were passing before him like dreams and his heart turned over at the sight of them.

The dark writhed around the souls of the lost children, clotting and loosening, so that for whole seconds he saw the pale figures crouching, then falling away. The witch's moaning became a piercing scream as he dug at the darkness inside her. She thrashed at the water like a ship struggling in a storm and he heard Merilee cry out in terror.

He glanced at the boiling waters of the lake. He saw the poor souls of the children peeling away, lying free on the surface like the transparent skins of an onion. Then they melted into the night, leaving small silver stains on the water.

His gaze scurried between them. He saw how the water became clear and pure where the silver touched, and moonlight dived down there, into the depths. But Merilee was crying behind him. And there were more souls, deep inside the witch where the dark hid. He searched and searched, wanting to free them, catching the hem of a cloak, a strand of hair, and then he saw the face that he'd been looking for. It almost stopped his heart.

A girl in a yellow cloak hovered at the edge of his vision. As he concentrated his light, swooping it over her, he saw a sprig of lavender in her hair.

"Laura!" he cried and she looked up and it was her.

But the dark was massing around even as he called her name, and the yellow cloak was fading. Other figures drifted past his eyes, reaching out, confusing him. His heart roared in his chest. Fear pounded through his veins. He felt his power weakening as the fog crept in at the sides of his eyes.

"She escaped me, son," his father's words came. "Slipped away like a stone from a peach."

The dark was numbing the outline of Laura. He was losing her.

"Are you afraid?" his father had asked him.

Now there was only the hem of the yellow cloak. He couldn't see the shape of her beneath it.

"You must become the thing for a moment yourself, in order to understand it."

Leo grasped at the scrap of yellow. But it kept slipping away, like water running into a crevice.

"That's where you can get lost—you must never lose your grip then."

For an instant, Leo saw the grief and defeat in his father's face. He remembered how strong he, Leo, had felt, how certain he'd been that he could right the world. He thought of Merilee, and the shutters opening, and how she'd seen the light of herself shining in between.

"How do you know if you can be a good wizard if you don't try?"

Leo knew that this moment—standing on this rock in the middle of the lake—was what he'd been waiting for all his life. This is who I am, he thought. This is what I'm for.

He hooked the yellow cloak with his vision and raked it in. The yellow deepened into gold. As he concentrated his gaze, the colors of Laura emerged, like the ripening of a sunrise. Her outline grew more certain. He saw the pale skin of her throat rising up from the collar, the hair swept up off her neck, and her eyes.

The power traveled like a lit fuse up the center of his body. He knew every bit of her—suddenly!—she was so clear for him, dazzling there under his gaze. He saw the little frozen girl inside her, and he took her, and laid her down in the palm of his mind, tight, like a pearl inside an oyster. He kept her, all of her, lying there in his mind and he pulled her towards him along the line of his vision. She was riding on the golden line, and he never let go, never relaxed a muscle, never thought of anything else but the whole of Laura.

A sound came from the shore, the roaring of a crowd that had gathered. The lake was screaming so that it seemed the sky would tumble, but still he reeled her in, not listening for anything but Laura's heartbeat.

And there now, in the water, she was struggling, her arms up, pearled with moonlit bubbles. She was reaching out and Merilee was running towards her, laughing, crying, shaking her head, calling and bending down on the hard rock, cutting her knees to shreds and pulling her own dear sister out of the lake, up into life.

When Leo touched her, she was still cold. Her skin was so pale it was translucent.

"Keep holding her," he told Merilee. He watched the moon sparkle on her as if she were made of glass. "Give her your warmth. Take her back over the rocks, along the top of the promontory, where she'll be safe."

"Come with me, please, Leo," begged Merilee.

But Leo had already turned back to the lake. He knew he wasn't finished.

The dark mass of the witch raged at him. She hulked against the sky, ravaged and bellowing. He could see no flicker of light in her now. She was empty of souls, and the terrible hunger in her moved over him, blinding him with her darkness.

Then the towering shape hollowed and he saw her seed and husk. He drew in his breath in terror.

Like corn rotting in the field, the core of her was a putrid black. It gathered all the darkness into itself, showing him a rage as deep as the lake. Leo shivered at the sight of it. What wickedness did Illuminato have in him that he could have created such a thing? This evil at her center had no voice; it was mute, contagious, feeding on souls. It seeped into Leo and he felt the blackness start in his own heart.

It stole up into his fingers and toes, a raging hatred. He thought of Beatrice, and how she'd spoilt his life and robbed him of love, and there she was in front of him now, the dark twisting into her exact shape, making her face come alive so that he wanted to dive into the lake and smash it for her. She laughed at him, snakes coiling on her head, her eyes flecking green. Then she poked her forked tongue out at him and he wanted to stab her to the heart.

Rage flooded him, filling him with poison. He hated Beatrice, he hated every living thing. He hated the earth, rain, wind, lightning, all things that were part of a world that dangled love before him and snatched it away. Most of all he, hated himself. In that moment, he knew, kneeling at the pit of darkness, that *this* was what Illuminato had felt all those years ago. Illuminato had drowned in this rage. He had surrendered.

"You must become the thing itself, before you can transform it. That's where you can get lost."

Leo leaned into the darkness. He wanted to let go, fall blind. Hatred throbbed through his veins. He closed his eyes. Behind his lids he found memories. Scenes from his childhood streamed like colored ribbons against the black. There was the cave where he had stood only hours ago. He remembered the glow of the stone wall, fragile now as a candle flame. But as he looked, he saw again the leaping animals within it, the ancient people, the beginnings of life. A tenderness arose in him for those living beings of long ago, and he remembered how Illuminato had once stood in the same place, showing his grandson these miracles of life. Illuminato, the man who could reveal a pulse beneath a cave wall, who could bring back life to a dying boy.

In that second, Leo felt at one with his ancestor, as if he had lived through every moment of Illuminato's life. He felt the power of his hatred, the enormity of his love. But he knew, too, that it was now he, Leo, who had to choose between them.

His toes crept back from the edge. He felt the hard, cool rock under the soles of his feet. And he let the living light of the cave fill his heart.

As he looked back at the lake, he saw the waves thrashing all around him. He gritted his teeth. He would watch and let it all pass in front of him, like a dream. And there, tall as the sky, he saw the shape of Beatrice swirling and stretching, changing into Francesca. She was chuckling as she threw dirt into a grave—his own. Leo's stomach clenched. But he didn't look away. He saw his mother running from him, a village burning, people clambering over the plague-ridden bodies of others, stealing their rings, their shoes, their clothes. There before him, the witch played out scenes of human cruelty and cowardice that he would never forget.

Leo watched with all his attention. He noticed every detail because he knew he would need it. Each illusion provided information to hold in his mind. Hours, minutes, the seed of Illuminato's evil twisted and grew into countless shapes and still he watched, holding fast to the edges of himself.

But it was enough to make you want to die. To never go back and belong to the human race. That is, if you became forever what you saw.

He felt very old, standing there on the rock. If he survived, he knew that, at least in his heart, he would never be the same again.

Leo had reached deep inside the seed. As he traveled further, the images began to blur, rushing past him so that he could hardly take them all in. He was approaching a nugget of dark that swept everything into itself. It painted no pictures, spoke no words. Whirling like a tornado, it expanded and shrank before him until, for just one moment, it held still.

His mind closed around it fast like a fist over a coin. It throbbed, a living thing, against the walls of his mind. The pain was searing—a blacksmith's hot iron on the skin. He couldn't hold it for long.

The only way was to transform it. "Then you'll be practicing the art of Metamorphosis, my boy!"

Leo was sweating all over his body. His heart thundered in his ears. The dark mass pulsed in his head. He tried to close his mind tighter. But his light was dimming. He knew he had to stop Illuminato's dark from spreading.

Under his feet was the cool gray rock. He imagined a stone in his hand. A piece of granite. He saw tiny crystals sparkling on its surface. He knew by heart, from all his study in the forest, the millions of grains of quartz and other minerals that lay inside.

He held the two things in his mind. The nugget of darkness and the stone. He looked at them both and understood every particle of their beings. His mind balanced them perfectly for a second, as if he were a scale, weighing them, judging them. And then the choice was easy, as easy as water flowing down a mountain. He opened the fold of dark in his mind and in that instant he slid the essence of his ancestor's evil into the stone.

A groan like the cracking of a mountain roared through the sky. The waters of the lake churned, sending up spray that leaped over Leo's head. He saw it sparkle as it shot through the air, then settled back on the surface of the lake in a patch of silver that glowed, for a moment, more brightly than the full moon.

Leo felt a gladness spread through his body. He looked down and saw the stone, a real piece of granite, in his hand. It had been born in his mind, and he fingered it now with amazement, examining its coarse-grained, grayish colored texture. It lay there in his palm unmoving, ordinary. The air sighed all around him, and Leo looked up from the stone and saw there above him, where the witch had been, it was as bright as day. The sky shimmered with the light of her soul released, and he was content.

He gazed out at the lake, gentle and smooth as glass. Then, still holding the stone, he turned and started the long climb over the rocks, back towards the people he loved.

Chapter Fifteen

On the night that Leo returned with the stone and the lake was set free, celebrations broke out in the piazza. The sky was alight with burning torches, but as the dawn came the villagers grew quiet, watching the sun rise over a new morning.

Marco had been amongst the crowd gathered at the shore that night. When Leo embraced him, it was as two grown men, father and son. Leo felt the line of his power reaching back in time and galloping forward, and he'd whispered, "Why didn't you ever tell me that it was Illuminato?"

"Why should a child start his life in shadow?" Marco had replied.

But then he'd begun to tell Leo, there on the pebbly shore, as the crowd drifted back to the village, about Manton, his father, and how he'd returned, raving, from the lake when Marco was only ten years old. Raving about the witch—the horror that Illuminato had created. "And I am his *son!*" Manton had wailed, and he'd started beating at himself, tearing at his skin so that Marco had to bind up his hands with cloth. They'd never gone back to the cave again. Those were the last words ever spoken between them.

"And Illuminato?" Leo had asked.

Marco had shrugged, helpless. "How can you justify evil? My grandfather was born with an unimaginable power. Blessed or cursed, whichever way you want to see it. He loved a woman who was not his wife. Loved her always, even when she married someone else. He kept his rage locked up, I suppose, like a monster in a cage. Until the day she wouldn't see him any more." Marco looked down. "Poor Caterina, *poverina.*"

Leo had brought out the stone then for Marco.

"We'll bury it, Leo," Marco told him. "Deep in the earth where stones belong. Only you and I know it exists, and when we die, it will exist no longer."

"Do you believe that, Papà? That if no one has knowledge of a thing, then it doesn't truly exist?"

But Marco had begun to sag against Leo, his breath rasping. He'd grabbed Leo's wrist. "When you were born and I saw what was inside you, I swore that you'd never walk in his shadow the way I did. I wanted you to use your powers proudly, and fulfill your destiny."

Leo had looked up at his father. "What did you see?"

"I think you know."

Leo had nodded then, smiling so that he'd felt his face might just split in two. For there, under the tiredness, the power of a lion was resting. It had helped him roar at the dark, and bring back life, and he could feel it still inside him, waiting, ready.

"Some things you only really believe when you discover them for yourself," Marco had said softly. "No one can tell you."

And Leo knew that it was true.

And so it was Leo who became keeper of the stone. He decided not to bury it as his father had suggested. In the past, too much had been buried. Too many secrets had been kept.

Leo knew he must always remember the path he didn't choose, the consequences of the dark.

So he took the stone and placed it in the cave. It lay there on the ledge, inside a carved wooden box that Aldo Butteri had given him on his thirteenth birthday. Leo didn't tell Aldo how he would use the box—Aldo might never have slept again!—so he just thanked him gracefully, and took it away.

Most days, Leo went down to the cave. He'd sit for a while, breathing in the salty air and the candle grease, gazing at the wall. He traveled very far in that place, and learned much, concentrating on the golden glow that now burned steadily inside him.

And when he was fifteen, Leo asked Merilee to marry him.

On a warm evening in July, Leo climbed down from his wedding carriage and stepped into the garden of Fiesole. He greeted the guests, thinking how much older he felt than his fifteen years. On the night that he'd returned with the stone, a weariness had come over him so that he could hardly lift one leg after the other. He'd stood still, looking at the crowd gathered on the shore, mesmerized by the flames leaping from their torches.

Leo remembered how Merilee had raced towards him, as if she couldn't get there fast enough. "Leo, did you know that you're *glowing*?" she'd whispered. "There are silver sparks all around your head."

Her eyes were wide open and her smile was generous. In that moment, he'd loved her more than at any time since they were born. He'd wanted to ask her to marry him then. But he felt very separate, too. The weariness overwhelmed him and he could have lain down there at her feet and slept for a year and a day.

That night, Leo had seen things that people knew only at the end of their lives. Some people never knew them. He'd seen the wickedness pass in front of his eyes and it had made him feel one hundred years old.

He'd held tight to Merilee's hand. She wouldn't ever know how it had been, out there on the rock, but they were born at the same moment, played together all their lives, and she was the only one who could bring the warmth back to his soul.

When Merilee told them of Leo's proposal, the Wise Women offered to hold the wedding feast there at Fiesole, where Laura had returned to study. Beatrice had become Laura's "companion and teacher," as she described it, responsible for looking after "the poor girl's health and education." Laura had come so far under her brilliant tutelage, she argued, it must be obvious that she was the only serious candidate now as Head. Brigida, who had stayed on as Head Wise Woman after the homecoming of Laura, said only, "There is time enough to think of these matters," and glided off to perform her duties.

As soon as Beatrice heard of the wedding, she began making lists. There was the food and the numbers of guests to be decided, and what of entertainment? Ever since the night of the Celebrations, Beatrice had undergone a mysterious change of attitude towards Leo. She would take charge, she told everyone, and prepare the best banquet ever to grace the halls of Fiesole.

A grand wedding table was set up in the Green Room.

The silken walls were festooned with flowers, and delicious aromas of sizzling meat and rice flavored the air. As Leo sat down at the head of the table, with Merilee at his side, he looked out over the table, rich with food and friends.

His father was sitting with Merilee's family— Francesca, Laura, and Franco. There was Marco's good friend Aldo Butteri and Signor Eco, and Isabella and her husband Alessandro. A sleepy baby called Rosa lay on Isabella's lap.

All around the room, the Wise Women of Fiesole sat at tables, talking. Beatrice hardly sat down, hovering over the tables like a hawk. She checked each dish as it was served, the quality of the wine, and Laura's health. "Don't catch cold now, dear," she urged, as she inspected a dish of rice. "I'll bring your cloak when we go out into the garden. These spring nights can be treacherous." She bent over Signor Eco's shoulder and whispered loudly, "Laura's still quite fragile, you know. Does too much, always planning some new course, writing that book of hers. If I didn't watch over her and make sure she was eating properly and getting some rest, she'd never manage. And then, of course, it's really *me* who has to keep the whole place running smoothly... Oh, well, I like to be useful. No one could say that I don't play my part!"

Isabella rolled her eyes at Leo. They had become

good friends. Isabella and her husband lived near Florence, on Alessandro's younger brother's estate. Leo would always feel grateful to Isabella because it was she who'd brought Marco to the lake that night. She had come to Merilee's village to ask for her help in seeking Alessandro, just as Beatrice had raised the alarm.

Leo raised his glass to Isabella. He remembered her first comment on meeting him. "Why Merilee, you never told me he was so handsome he *glowed!*" He reddened now, just thinking of it.

"Hey you, husband!" Merilee reached over and pinched his cheek.

"Give us a song, Meri!" Aldo Butteri called out from across the table.

Merilee, who never needed much urging these days, took out her recorder. Aldo tapped his glass for quiet and into the space of held breaths and half-finished conversations Merilee's dance tune leaped and skipped. She tapped her foot as she played, jigging amongst the tables, and people clapped their hands to the rhythm as the cutlery at their elbows jumped and the wine trembled in the glasses.

Leo watched, grinning. He looked at the people's faces, many from his village, and thought how different they seemed. More open, less fearful, *happy*. He remembered the night, three years ago, when the villagers had come up to him, one by one. They'd touched his hair, still sparkling with wizard-light. They'd taken his hand and kissed it.

"We will never forget this," Fabbio had told him.

"And we will never tell," another promised.

A loud burst of laughter came from Leo's right. Marco and Aldo were locked in battle over something and Francesca threatened to pour wine over Aldo's head.

"*Va bene*," Signor Butteri surrendered gracefully. "I'll bow to the good sense of a lady." He poured them all another cup of wine and slapped Marco on the back. "Drink up, old friend, it'll improve your digestion and nourish your blood."

Marco clinked his glass with Aldo's and drank.

When Merilee came back to the table, after many bows and cheering, Signor Butteri remarked to her, "With your talent, you'll soon be playing at court."

"She is already," cried Leo, "next month. For the Duke of Urbino, no less."

Aldo shook his head in wonder. "What a blessed pair you are. And isn't it good to see your papà doing so well?" Signor Butteri leaned close to Leo. Quickly he touched the iron of the table leg for luck. "It's the wine that does it, I believe. That, and the purifying waters of the lake."

Leo and Marco grinned at each other.

Aldo Butteri was convinced that the waters of the lake now had healing properties. Every morning you could see him wading in, his hose and shoes neatly piled on the pebbly shore behind him. He swore it did his legs good, and he could stand at the bench of his shop for much longer now, after he'd had a good soak in the crystal waters of the lake. Who knew, Leo thought, maybe it was true.

Sometimes Aldo would persuade Marco to come with him to the lake and they'd wade together in the water, watching the miracle of little fishes darting around their legs. In summer, with the day's work finished, people from the village brought picnics of cheese and wine down to the lake for supper, and the children paddled at the edge.

Suddenly overcome by good fortune, friends, and the warmth of his favorite wine, Aldo Butteri stood up and made a toast. "Here's to young Leo Pericolo, savior of the lake. Our blessings to you and your new wife—good health and *tanti bambini!*"

Leo and Merilee stood up, raising their glasses to all the company.

In that moment, with love brimming inside him like the wine in his glass, Leo felt prepared for whatever may happen next.

About the Author

ANNA FIENBERG gets her ideas from her own dreams, people she meets, snatches of overheard conversation. She always carries a notebook with her in case she hears something interesting.

Anna likes to live in books as well as real life. She was once editor of *School Magazine*, where she read over a thousand books a year. She wrote plays and stories for the magazine and then began writing her own books. She has written award-winning picture books, short stories, junior novels, and fiction for teenagers and young adults.

Anna Fienberg lives in Australia.